Powell Place

Shawn Powell

CONTENTS

THE BENIFICIARY

Some of her friends told her that she was being vindictive. "You can't help who you fall in love with," she would reply.

"Not even if he's already married?"

Nope, not even if they were already married.

Renae knew that to be true firsthand. These were the exact words that her ex-husband had told her before he closed the front door of their home and walked out on her and their seven-year-old daughter's lives forever. Of course, those words about not controlling who you fall in love with held no weight with her at that exact moment. But she had never forgotten them. Probably the coldest choice of words a husband could ever tell his wife before walking out.

As the years passed and the realization that her husband wasn't ever coming back began to set in, she had become a tad bitter. What woman wouldn't be after such a traumatizing dismissal? The pain of him being gone lurked even after two years had passed, but what had really consumed her was the drastic lifestyle change she had to make. He had been the primary bread winner, and although she had gotten a small settlement amount after the divorce, eventually the bills began to pile up and she could no longer maintain the same lifestyle she had enjoyed while being married.

Together, they had lived in a three-bedroom house. After he left, she had to down grade to a one-bedroom apartment on the lower East Side. Her clothing had always been designer, her car was always the current year's model. Now, her car was seven years old, she still wore designer clothing, but she made it last a lot longer.

By the time she met Matt, she was well over her past marriage, and free to mingle. Her daughter, now eighteen, had just finished high school, had a steady boyfriend, and was on her way to college. She had done her job as a parent, and now she was looking to rekindle what her prior husband had stripped from her, love.

The affair started at the office.

Renae had always noticed that he was attractive and that he was kind. She could tell by the way he interacted with the employees. Everyone, from the janitor to the office manager, got the same respect from Matt. Whenever there was a company meeting or outing, oddly enough, she always found herself seated at his table or on his side of the conference room. She quickly recognized that if they were ever in the same room, she would always be close enough to him so that she could smell the exact fragrance of cologne that he wore on a given night. If ever there was a project, he made her the lead manager. Sure, her talents and educational accolades spoke for themselves, but she still felt drawn to him. He was attractive, important, powerful, successful…

…and married.

She remembered the first time she asked him to lunch. She was intimidated, but two years had passed with only the assumption that something could be brewing between them. She had admired him the entire while, waiting, or wanting him to make the first move. That time hadn't come in two years, so she changed her strategy. She assumed that asking him to lunch wouldn't raise any immediate red flags. Still, she had to know if he paid as much attention to her as she paid to him. She figured that the gesture of asking him to lunch would lead to something. She could feel it, and if she could feel it, he had to feel it too. She caught up with him near the elevators around noon, and hopped on it with him. He was happy to see her, he even pulled her in for a quick shoulder hug.

"What are you doing for lunch?" he asked her.

She was dumbfounded, she had made all the plans and had finally built up the nerve to ask him to lunch, and before she could open her mouth, he had asked her. That was a sign.

They ended up at a small sandwich shop two blocks away from the office building they worked in. While they ate their chicken Caprese paninis, everything was as cordial as could be expected between two co-workers. By the time their lunch had finished, Renae had resolved that she had to do more. She still wasn't sure that he felt the same connection that she felt. So, before the day ended, she had texted him asking him to have dinner with her that same evening. He didn't reply.

For the rest of that day she was in the dumps. She could handle the rejection, but the embarrassment of being rejected by a married man brewed a serious feeling of regret. How could she tell her friends that she had pursued a married man, and that he had rejected her advances?

At 8PM that evening, her phone buzzed while she lay in her bed flipping aimlessly through the television channels. She picked up the phone from the nightstand and read the text. It was Matt, and the text read, "What are you doing now?"

She swallowed hard and held the cellphone close to her chest. She was flattered. "Nothing," she texted back, swiftly.

Then, her phone rang, and it was him. They agreed to meet at the Rooftop café downtown for drinks that evening. Renae dressed in a flash and on her way out she passed her daughter and her boyfriend who were both sitting on the couch in the Livingroom. Her daughter eyed her from the couch. "Where you going?" she asked. She hadn't seen her mom so jazzed up in ages.

"I got a date," Renae replied, grabbing her jacket from the coat closet and twirling out the front door.

Renae and Matt had sex that same night. She had assumed everything correctly. Matt did have a connection with her, and yes, he had purposely kept her in his closest working circles. He explained that his relationship with his wife hadn't been anything more than cordial for the last three years. They drank multiple rounds of scotch that evening, and he got a room in the Plaza hotel two blocks away. They walked to the hotel room hand in hand. The connection was instant, she felt as if she had known him for years, and well technically she had.

Matt didn't stay with her the entire night, but she woke up alone in the plush hotel room still feeling extremely optimistic. It had taken a while, but she could see the future again. She longed for the sumptuous life she had had 10 years before. Love was in the air.

That was how the relationship began. True to Matt's words, he did get a divorce, and it only took six months for it to become final. Renae made him marry her almost immediately, and just four months after his divorce was final he flew her to Vegas and they got married at a small chapel. Just the two of them, and her daughter.

The challenges began almost as quickly. The first confrontation came when he asked her to quit her job. Not only did he not want to work in the same office as his wife, he didn't want his wife to work at all. Worse than that, he refused to work with her on any of her ideas for compromise. Not even agreeing to letting her start her own business. Now she feared not being able to make money to support herself. What if he left? The thought made her shiver inside.

She thought that she had survived the trauma of being abandoned. Yet, something as simple as not being able to work haunted her spirit. Whereas most women would probably relish the idea of being a house wife, it worried her. They had no kids together; his kids were teenagers and lived with his ex-wife. At least she would be able to go and come as she pleased, yet, that reasoning was not enough to put her at ease. She knew how easy it was for men to walk out on their wives. She had been left before, and even her new husband had just left his. She was worried, worried that things were moving way too fast.

Matt demanded that she quit, and did everything short

of firing her. The next hurdle came when it was time to find a place for both of them to live. Matt didn't take any of her ideas into consideration, he found a two-story contemporary home deep in the suburbs and left her there. He went to work every day and she stayed at home. He gave her what he thought she should have and not what she asked for. The remoteness of her new home caused a great deal of depression and isolation for her, and her daughter.

Tiffany complained about the distance daily. She had a boyfriend who didn't drive, and public transportation didn't come to where they lived now. So, after about four months she and her boyfriend began to despise Matt. They had been a part of the relationship since it began. They remembered how happy Renae had been up until the marriage. They hated that she wasn't the same exuberant personality anymore. They hated that they went from being with each other daily to only on the weekends. More than that, Tiffany had witnessed the turmoil her mother had gone through before. She had been there since the beginning of her mother's struggles. She too was standing at the exact door that her mother stood in when her father slammed it on his way out. She too had suffered.

Now everything was going in reverse.

Renae thought that she could tough it out. She told Tiffany that things would get better, that the first year of marriage was always the hardest. Yet, after a year of marriage, things had only gotten worse. It seemed that she and Matt had a better relationship when they were just co-workers. Matt was a workaholic and spent more time at the office than he did at home. He would work most days until 9PM, and by the time he got home, he was exhausted, and went to sleep. The likelihood that they would be intimate was in the low percentile. When she tried to talk to him about the outrageous amount of time he spent in the office, he would reply, "That's how I was when you met me. Now it's a problem?"

After the first year, she, for the first time, began to put herself in Matt's ex-wife's shoes. She began to understand some of the issues that had probably led to their divorce. Renae felt isolated from the world, left with only her thoughts, and her thoughts were all negative. Tiffany was her only comfort, the only one who truly understood her position, because she had lived it with her. One evening she and Tiffany had a conversation about how to get Matt to be a more understanding person. Together, they had come up with an idea. They would have lunch with Matt and try to get him to understand how they felt. Hoping that approaching him as a team would force him to listen. They high fived at the idea.

Renae called Matt to set up a lunch date, letting it be known that the lunching would be to discuss family issues. Matt seemed enthused at the idea of a meeting. He promised to free his schedule so that the idea could become a reality. The reality was that he would never make time. It took Renae and Tiffany only two months to understand that.

One day Tiffany invited her mother and her boyfriend Edgar to a family meeting. Edgar, Tiffany, and Renae sat around the glass dining room table in the home that she shared with Matt. Edgar had become like a son to her over the last two years. She kind of admired how he treated her daughter, and she embraced their relationship as if they were already married. Tiffany began the meeting by telling her mother that Edgar had important news to share, and it wasn't good. Renae immediately pushed her chair back away from the table and crossed the kitchen to pick up the bottle of red wine on the counter. She grabbed a wine glass from a rack and poured a glass before sitting back down with the two of them.

"Mom," Tiffany began. "I listen to you complain about Matt every day, all day. I will never forget the way you looked when dad walked out on us." Her voice began to break as she continued. "So, I made a promise to myself

9

on that day to make sure that you wouldn't be hurt again."

Renae swigged her wine, then swirled the glass. She glanced over at Edgar whose head was hung. "What is it?" she asked, blandly.

"I had Edgar follow Matt one night," Tiffany continued before she looked to Edgar. "Do you want to tell her the rest?" she asked him.

"I followed him one day after he got off work," Edgar began, never lifting his eyes from the tiled floor. "I saw him meet with another woman. They walked to a restaurant not far from the building he works in. I hung around outside since I wasn't dressed up enough to get in. They came out about an hour later, and he kissed her before she got in her cab."

Renae finished her wine. "When was this?" she asked without emotion.

Edgar finally looked up. "About a week ago. Look, I really didn't want to get involved, but I love Tiffany and I love you. So, when Tiffany asked me to help... I'm sorry to have to tell you this." He dropped his head again.

"What type of kiss was it, Edgar?" she asked, her emotions still in check.

Edgar looked up and in her eyes. He nodded his head up and down solemnly. "That kind of kiss," he said.

Renae stood up and calmly walked over to the sink with her wine glass. The room was silent. Then suddenly, she slammed the glass down into the sink, shattering the tranquility of the room.

Tiffany got up and rushed to her aid.

Renae began to sob hysterically. Her nose ran, and she dropped to the floor. "Why?!" she screamed out. Tiffany sat on the floor cradling her mother's head in her arms. They sat on the floor crying together for near 30 minutes. When Renae's tears began to slow, Tiffany whispered in her ear. "Me and Edgar have a plan momma."

Renae didn't really care to hear about any plans. She knew that she had to stand up and be strong for her daughter, though. So, she gathered herself and walked to the guest bathroom. She splashed her face with sink water and used a hand towel to dry it. Her mascara stained her face where the tears had run, and she was incredibly weak.

She sat on the closed toilet with her face in her palms. She pondered whether to confront Matt or not. She still felt she needed more information. More evidence. Her instincts had alerted her to something like this about three months earlier. She had been through it before, so she knew the signs. How much more information did she need before he just walked out. She didn't want to waste any more time trying to love a man who didn't want to be loved. She needed to find another job, another apartment, of course she would have to downgrade her living arrangement again…. There was so much to think about.

Then she remembered her daughter had spoken of a plan. Suddenly, she was attentive. She got herself together and went back into the kitchen. Edgar and Tiffany both stared at her, their eyes showing concern. "I'm ok guys," she said flatly before sliding into her chair. "So, what's this plan?" she asked.

Tiffany stood up and adjusted her blouse. She walked over to her mother and held her face in between both her palms. "I love you mommy, so much," she began. She kissed her before walking over to Edgar's chair and sitting in his lap. "We don't want to see you have to go through any suffering like you went through last time with dad. You don't deserve it. You don't deserve to always get the short end of the stick. That's why we came up with a plan to make sure that when this is over, at least you're taken care of."

Renae was confused. She couldn't think of anything either of them could do to make this go away. She didn't even know if she wanted to divorce, or to try and work it out. There was so much to think about.

"Edgar, tell her the plan," she heard her daughter say, pulling her from her thoughts.

Edgar was soft spoken. With Tiffany sitting in his lap, he spoke from behind her back, almost like he was hiding. "Your husband has an insurance policy, I heard it's worth a lot. I could make sure you collect on it," he said. He was talking more to the floor than to her directly.

Renae was sure she heard him correctly, but she couldn't look him in his eyes to see if he was serious. Renae recalled sitting on the patio chatting with Tiffany about the million-dollar life insurance policy Matt had taken out. He had told her that she would be the beneficiary if something happened to him. Renae began to conjure up the idea of being a millionaire. A million dollars! She would be secure for the rest of her life. Maybe start that business she always wanted to start. Do some traveling...

Her mind jolted back to the reality of sitting in the kitchen with her daughter's boyfriend, who had just offered to murder her husband.

Tiffany stood up again. "If and when he leaves, mom, you're going to be left with nothing! Was this all part of his plan?!" she ranted. "He made you quit your job only so that he could woo other women without you seeing!" Tiffany shouted. "You don't deserve to go backwards anymore because of a man. Move forward, mom! Let us help you!" Tiffany exclaimed. She did everything but jump up and down in the middle of the floor.

Renae was baffled. Not so much by the proposition, but because nothing in her mind told her that the conversation was inappropriate. She vaguely heard Tiffany's explanation for going through with something as wacky as murder for hire. She could have saved her voice. The idea was perfect from the moment it spilled from Edgar's mouth. She didn't want to participate in an extensive conversation about murdering her husband, and she didn't want to seem easily persuaded. So, she quietly got up and crossed the room for the stairs. She left them in the dining room and went to her bedroom and lay down.

She was overwhelmed with emotions and she needed to rest.

When she woke up, Matt was coming into the bedroom. She watched him from under her covers. The nightstand clock read 1AM. Her eyes began to water. Wasn't that much work in the world. She watched as he undressed, undeterred. He really didn't care about her, she knew how this would play out. She would beg him for more attention, make accusations about where he was and what he'd been doing. He would deny everything and accuse her of nagging, and eventually he would just leave. Leave her to pick up the pieces and fend for herself. She thought to confront him about the allegations Tiffany and Edgar had charged against him. She didn't. Matt undressed, brushed his teeth and slid into bed, his back to hers, no kiss, no hug, no affection.

When she woke up the next morning, she made him breakfast and served him coffee. She sat down across the table from him and watched him while he read his cell phone. He looked up after a moment, "What?" he asked.

She didn't want to bombard him with accusations as if she knew something, so, with a steady voice, she said, "I just want to know why you feel its ok to come home at 1AM?"

"Gotta work to pay the bills baby," he said promptly. That said, he finished his everything bagel, grabbed his briefcase and headed in to work. He didn't even kiss her.

Renae sat at the dining room table with her head down in despondence. She felt her daughter's arms around her a short moment later. She began to sob as her daughter comforted her with her embrace. "I want to go through with it," Renae said, her voice breaking after every word.

Her daughter squeezed her hard. "No worries mommy," she whispered in her ear. "I'll take care of him. We won't be left with nothing this time."

Renae didn't know how the murder would take place. She feared having to play some part in the entire ordeal, but Tiffany had never asked or told her anything.

For two days her husband came and went like everything was normal. Renae figured that maybe, her daughter and Edgar had decided against going through with the crime. She didn't know how to feel about that. As the days passed, she began to look forward to Matt's demise. She looked forward to living not just comfortably, but fabulously without dependence on a man.

Then, on Saturday afternoon, as she lay in bed watching Lifetime, her cellphone rang. She didn't recognize the number, yet instinctively she knew something wasn't right. She looked at the number on her screen for three rings before she finally answered. Her heart was beating fast, and her stomach churned.

It was a detective. They told her that her husband had been stabbed to death in a restaurant bathroom. She was summoned to the coroner's office to identify the body. Her reaction was genuine. She sat up and gasped. "Oh my god!" she screamed. The detective was silent on the other line while he waited for Renae to calm down a bit. After three minutes of crying and questions, she had calmed enough for the detective to give her the coroner's address. When Renae hung up, she dressed in jeans and a sweatshirt and donned heavy black shades. She hadn't heard from Tiffany yet and thought it too soon to reach out. She was truly heart broken, she was going to miss Matt. She hadn't wanted to lose him in any fashion, but it was inevitable that they were going to part. At least now she wouldn't get the short end of the stick.

She arrived at the coroner's and identified the body. It was a horrible sight, no one questioned her sincerity as she cried profusely and crumpled to the cold cement floor. What she hadn't anticipated was seeing his mutilated body. He had been stabbed 14 times. The detective met her at the coroner's office, a weathered-faced white man with a towering presence. He walked with her as she made her way out of the coroner's office, he explained that Matt had fought to the end. They even had footage of the perpetrator leaving the restaurant. Renae panicked a little. Footage?

The detective said they were investigating the case thoroughly and would be in constant touch with her as the case continued. Before she parted from the detective, she did have one question. "Was he alone at the restaurant?" she asked.

The detective shook his head no. "He had been having lunch with a co-worker at the time," the Detective explained. "She did make a statement and promised to assist with the investigation."

"She." The word echoed throughout her skull. "Who is she?" she asked.

"She identified herself as a co-worker," the detective stated. He looked Renae directly in her eyes. "Do you know of anybody who could have done this? I mean, although his wallet is missing, this seems to be a little more than a botched robbery. The multiple stab wounds tell a different story." He waited for her response. She didn't know what to say initially. She was still lost over the fact that he was having lunch with a female "co-worker."

"No," she said. "He never led me to believe that he had any issues with anyone."

The detective just stared at her for a long moment. "Not a problem. If you think of anything, or anyone, feel free to call me." He handed her a business card.

Renae drove home in tears and with mixed emotions. It was depressing to know that while she lay at home distraught about her relationship, he was out wining and dining another woman. He was gone now, and at least she could prepare for a financially secure future.

Tiffany and Edgar were already at the house when she got there. They all sat around the dining room table. The room was somber, but the talk of the insurance policy soon changed the vibe of the room. They didn't talk much about the process it took to kill Matt. Renae did notice that

Edgar's hand was bandaged. They talked about how both Edgar and her daughter would be compensated for their work. Renae agreed to give them two hundred thousand dollars to pay for their wedding and to begin their new life wherever they chose. Just like that, the marriage was over.

Renae spent the rest of the evening alone. She couldn't sleep. She was torn between grieving and prosperity. She was that way the entire weekend, and by the time Monday rolled around she had made her first appointment to meet with the life insurance holders. Thursday afternoon she was in their downtown offices. She had decided that she would send Matt off in style. The funeral would be extravagant, it was the least she could do.

She took the elevators of the towering glass building up to the 12th floor and signed in at the front desk, verifying her appointment. After a ten-minute wait, a tan slender woman appeared from the rear and introduced herself. Renae followed her to her office.

In the office Renae took a seat in front of the rustic executive desk. The insurance adjuster sat behind the desk, pulled a folder from a drawer and placed it on the desk top. "Mrs. Sanders," the adjustor began. "I understand that you are here in behalf of your now deceased husband. Matthew Sanders."

Renae naturally choked up at the thought of Matthew having passed. She could still see his wounded body lying on the cold steel table. She nodded to the adjuster.

The adjuster opened the folder and looked over a few documents. Her facial expression began to change the more she read. Then finally she looked up, "Who is Jessica Sanders?" she asked.

Renae briefly thought. She had heard Matt mention the name before. Then she recalled that Jessica was his ex-wife. "I believe that Jessica is his former wife," she said flatly, still pondering why her name was being mentioned. She watched as the insurance adjusters' brow crinkled. "Is there a problem?" Renae asked.

The insurance adjuster didn't answer, she used her highlighter to mark something in the folder. Then she spun the folder around on the desk for Renae to read. Renae's eyes scrolled the page from the top her eyes landing on the highlighted area near the bottom. She saw her husband's signature, and just below that, listed as the beneficiary was Jessica Sanders, his ex-wife.

All the breath left Renae's body. She re-read the name nine times before she spun the folder back around to the adjuster. "So, what? What does that mean?" she asked, abruptly. She felt her body temperature rise; it was instantly warm in the room. She had a slight dizzy spell, even as she asked the question she had already reasoned what it meant.

The adjuster cleared her throat to buy time, this was the most awkward situation she had ever been in as an adjuster. "I'm afraid it means that his ex-wife is still the beneficiary of the policy."

Renae stood up quick, her chair tumbling backwards. "But what does that mean!?" she shouted.

The adjuster leaned back in her chair. She was prepared to move swiftly if things got out of hand. "It means you have no authority to collect on the insurance claim. I'm sorry."

Renae snatched the folder off the desk and tore up the papers inside and tossed them into the air. The torn papers slowly floated to the floor. "That doesn't make any sense! I'm his wife! I'm the fucking beneficiary!" she refuted.

The claims adjuster stood up now. "I think you need to leave, Mrs. Sanders. There is nothing more I can do for you here," she said calmly, already walking towards the door.

She opened the door and Renae turned around and stormed out. She struggled to put one foot in front of the other. She made it out the office and found the nearest restroom. Inside the bathroom she found a stall locked the door and sat down on the toilet. She braced her hands against each of the stalls walls to steady herself. She was dizzy and on the verge of passing out.

It was only the buzzing of her phone that helped steady her. She slowly let go of the wall and pulled her cellphone from her purse. It was a text from her daughter. She unlocked the screen and read the text.

Edgar had been arrested.

She was no longer dizzy. She gathered her wits, picked up her purse and left the bathroom. She hopped on the elevator and the dizziness returned. When the doors of the elevator opened, the detective she had met at the morgue was waiting for her along with two uniformed officers. The detective smiled when he saw her. "Just the person we have been looking for," he said, his voice dripping sarcasm. The two uniformed officers quickly placed her under arrest while reading her rights. They ushered her to and out the revolving doors of the building. They put her in the back of a police cruiser and sped away for the city jail.

It was the DNA left from Edgar's wounded hand during the scuffle that led them to him. His blood was left in the restroom along with Matt's. When they caught up with Edgar at his home, he was with his girlfriend, who just so happened to be Renae's daughter. It was Edgar's statements that the detective used to get an arrest warrant for Renae, and it was bad planning overall that foiled the likely hood of her ever receiving a penny of the life insurance policy.

You can't control who you fall in love with. Jessica Sanders understood that perfectly. As she checked her bags in at the airport she thought about how blessed she was, and about the misfortune of Renae. She needed to take a vacation to free her mind from the tragic events that had consumed her since her divorce. She was on her way to visit Spain, then France, Ghana. Australia, Japan………..

DREAM DRUGS

It was two months after the accident when Josh realized that he had insomnia. It was an atrocious crash that left the car totaled. Josh was the passenger, and his best friend Lou was the driver. They were leaving a Frat party, and they were wasted. Driving home from the party, Lou lost control of the wheel while doing 90 miles per hour on a sharp curve. The car left the road, was air borne for two seconds, then tumbled down an embankment and landed on its side in a ditch. Josh didn't remember any of this, he had only been told the story by friends and family. Lou wasn't so lucky; he had broken his neck and died. Josh had been in a coma for three days after the crash, and after that, he spent another month in the hospital in rehabilitation. He had been home from the hospital two months now, and he was averaging two hours sleep in a 24 hour timespan.

Outside of Lou, Josh is a loner. He is a 21-year-old chemical biology major, and this is his sophomore year in college. He still lives with his mother. When he finally went back to school, he was welcomed back to the campus like a war hero. Everyone had heard about the tragedy, he had even made the evening news. This was the most popular he had ever been in his entire life. It was sad that it was under these circumstances.

The high of his return to school wore off quickly, and in no time he was just another person on campus. Now and then someone would point at him in passing while they told the story of "the accident", but things were back to normal. Except, he couldn't sleep. He would go to bed every night around 12AM, then he would toss and turn until 5AM, leaving him with only two hours of sleep. Most days his eyes were blood shot, and the bags under them were fuller than a homeless person's cart. He often nodded off in classes, and it was beginning to affect his studies. It was when he began to hallucinate that he knew he had to seek treatment.

He returned to the doctor who cared for him during his stay in the hospital. His doctor told him that insomnia was normal due to the trauma sustained from the car accident, not to mention the loss of his friend. The doctor told Josh that there was no known cure for insomnia, but he did prescribe him sleeping pills. Josh left and filled his prescription immediately. The sleeping pills didn't work well, instead of falling asleep at 5AM, he was falling asleep at 4AM. He returned to his doctor again after a week's time. This time, the doctor recommended him to a psychiatrist.

Josh had high expectations as he lay down on the chaise lounge in the psychiatrist's office. He knew that the bulk of his problem was mental, there were a lot of thoughts that coursed his mind during those sleepless nights. Maybe he could have done more to prevent the events that led up to the car accident. At times, he felt like he was responsible for the entire night. He explained his feelings to the psychiatrist. The psychiatrist made it clear that this was normal and would subside. He prescribed a stronger sleeping pill and weekly counseling sessions. Still, none of this worked.

One morning at 3AM, Josh was awake watching a documentary on heroin abuse. He was amused by the way they would nod off when they got high. They were going to sleep. The wheels in his brain began to churn. In fact, he didn't sleep at all that evening, nor was he tired, because he had an idea. When he got to school that morning, he skipped the first class and headed to the library. He spent two hours in the library engaged in an extensive study on sleeping pills and insomnia. Then, he researched the active ingredients that made sleeping pills potent, and did in-depth research on heroin. He ended up not attending any classes that day, and by 5PM he was leaving with over one hundred printed pages.

The next day Josh called Lance, the campus drug supplier. No matter what the drug, Lance had access to it. He was a lanky guy with long, stringy blonde hair and a gaunt face. He looked like he used more drugs than he sold. They met at the school's gym, and it was here, at the very top of the bleachers, that Josh gave Lance a list of drugs for him to secure. Lance was a little confused by the names of some the drugs on the list, all of which he had never even heard of. It wasn't like Lance not to supply to those in need. Besides, he was well connected, and he had a reputation to maintain. This is what made him the success he was.

He told Josh it would take a week, and that he had to charge him extra because what he was asking for wasn't common, but he was sure he could get everything on the list. Then, as an afterthought, he asked Josh why. Why did he need such a creative list of dope? Josh explained that since the accident he hadn't been sleeping well, that he had insomnia, and that there wasn't a sleeping pill strong enough to medicate him. Now, he needed the drugs in their rawest form just for them to have an effect. Lance listened, semi-amused. He wasn't sure what insomnia was, he shrugged as a matter of fact. Lance, just like everyone else around campus, knew Josh was weird anyway.

True to his word, before the week was up, Lance pulled Josh into the gym's bathroom and gave him seven different baggies with various powders in each one. They were labeled individually with colored stickers. Lance read the label on each baggie as he handed them to Josh. Josh promptly paid him 300 dollars, stashed the drugs in his backpack, and left.

The next evening, when the school's lab was empty, Josh went in and set up shop. He had separated his ingredients at home and measured them out. In the lab, he mixed all the ingredients in a pill press, added corn starch as a filler, added xanthan gum to act as a binder, and gellan gum to help the stomach break the pill up with a tiny bit of shellac to coat the pills. He pressed the pills in the press, and out popped a tiny blue pill. He held the pill up to the light to examine it, and it looked like any other pill he had ever seen. He pressed out nine more pills, cleaned up the lab, packed up his supplies swiftly, and left.

At 9PM that evening, he took the pill. In 15 minutes he was drowsy. Five minutes after that, he was sleep. The next thing Josh knew, his alarm clock was blaring in his ear, and it was 6AM. Unbelievably, he had slept the entire night through. He could feel the difference as soon as his feet touched the floor, he was energized. He felt new, excited to live, explosive even. By the time he started to brush his teeth, he began to remember his dream. He smiled while he brushed and he relived portions of his dream. He could still feel and remember the dream as if it was a recent real-life occurrence. It was quite clearly the best dream ever.

He caught the city bus to school, and the entire forty-minute ride, he was still reliving his dream. In his dream he was a world-renowned scientist, popular and well respected in his field. He was such a success that he lived in a ten-bedroom mansion. He was a bachelor, and his girlfriend was a swimsuit model. He was a celebrity of sorts, everywhere he went, people would ask for his autograph and a selfie, or they would just record him on their cell phones. His claim to fame was inventing a drug that could add 20 years to one's life. It was the invention of this life enhancing pill that made him famous, and a multi-billionaire in his dream. Josh didn't know what gave him the better feeling, the fact that he was well rested or the dream.

The very next night, he took the pill again. The process was the same, he fell asleep in 20 minutes. What was more interesting than the night before was that his dream began exactly where it had left off. It was the second-best dream he ever had, only comparable to the first time he had taken the pill. After the third night, he was absolutely living another life in his head, and it felt real. It got to the point where he wanted to go home to nap in the middle of the day, just because life was better for him in dream world. In his dreams, he was everything that he wasn't in real life, and no matter where the dream ended, the next time he fell asleep, the dream would pick up exactly where it left off. He wanted to tell someone. So, before he left school that day, he called Lance and set up a meeting at the gym.

Josh figured if he had to tell someone, then it should be Lance. Not because Lance would care about how well he slept, but this could also be lucrative. It was ironic to him that he was a renowned scientist in his dream life, credited for inventing a life enhancing drug, and in the real world he could achieve almost the same success because of a drug he invented. Later that day, he met up with Lance at the top of the bleachers. He gave Lance a small blue pill and told him to take it before he went to bed. Lance asked him if the pill had a name. Josh simply replied, "Dreamers". Lance, the avid drug user that he was, did not have any other questions. He took the pill that very night.

When Lance dreamed, he dreamed he was the most notorious drug kingpin the United States had ever seen. He was untouchable. The Feds couldn't touch him, even though they tried. He had multiple mansions, sports cars, a yacht, and a myriad of women. He would deliver drugs by the pounds state to state by means of his private jet. Anyone who could be a problem was on his payroll, from his personal pilot, to some members of the TSA. In his dream, he was everything that he wanted to be in real life. Lances dream was lively and entertaining, like a movie and a video game intertwined, he had just as much control of his actions as he did in real life.

Lance was so well rested, he jogged to school the next day. The entire three miles. When he saw Josh, their eyes locked. It was clear that the experience for them both was identical. They had slept well. Lance animatedly explained his dream in graphic detail as they headed for their third class, and Josh shared his dreams. Lance demanded another pill, he took it that night, and true to Josh's words, his dream had picked up exactly where it had left off. Lance woke up the next morning with dollar signs in his eyes. The lives that they were living in their dreams could become real. Lance was addicted.

They met at the gym again, Lance had an idea to throw a party to introduce the drug to his customers, and Josh thought it was a grand idea. He immediately saw himself living the life he lived in his dreams. This time, Lance supplied the drugs free of charge, and Josh pressed out 20 pills. He gave all 20 to Lance. It had been four days since Josh invented the dreamer, and only now did it occur to him that he had not went to bed sober since the first day he took the pill. That night, he tried to sleep without taking the pill. It was back to normal, he couldn't sleep, and he tossed and turned until he was irritated. Yet, he was determined to make it through the night without popping a dreamer, he stayed committed, and at 4:26AM he fell asleep.

That night when Josh dreamed, he dreamed that a patient had taken the drug he had invented and died. Then, the nightmare began. The media was in a fury, the family of the victim was on every news station and so was his face. People picketed outside his mansion, they threw rocks at him while he was in the streets, and he had to hire security.

Even before his dream ended, two more people had passed because of his drug. He was receiving death threats by phone and on social media. Then he got arrested, and while in jail his girlfriend left him for a pro football player, and even this was on the news. Everything that was good in his previous dreams was failing now, nothing was going his way, and he even contemplated suicide.

Josh never heard his alarm go off. He suddenly woke up. He sat up quick, he was drenched in sweat and shivering, cold and hot simultaneously. Immediately, he recognized this as a side effect, severe withdrawal symptoms. In one night, and with less than three hours sleep, he had the worst dream he had ever had in his life. The clock on his night stand read 8AM. He was late for school.

He was brutally tired that day, like he hadn't slept in days. To go to sleep without taking a dreamer, conclusively, was a nightmare. The nightmare stayed on Josh's mind that entire day. He hadn't considered that there would be a side effect to the drug. Understandable though, since side effects were common with any drug. He cursed himself for overlooking this attribute.

He ran into Lance later that day, in the common area. Lance was still motivated. All he could talk about was how great his dreams were, and the party that he had planned. He handed Josh a fold of money. Lance had already sold the last twenty pills. He also gave Josh a blue lunch box. He told him to make 100 pills. Josh looked at the money, amused. He had almost forgotten that there was money involved.

Josh asked Lance if he had been to sleep without out taking a dreamer yet. Lance eyed him incredulously, he didn't understand why he would. Dreamers made sleep worth sleeping. Josh explained that he had tried going to sleep without one, and the experience wasn't the greatest. Lance had a simple solution, take another dreamer.

At home in his room Josh opened the lunch box, revealing enough dope for 100 pills. He counted out the money. It totaled 500 dollars. A quick estimate revealed that Lance had to be selling the pills for at least 50 dollars apiece. At this rate, they would be rich in less than a year. Maybe Lance was right, why worry about the side effects? A bad dream had never killed anyone.

That night, Josh took a dreamer. When he fell asleep, all that had gone bad in the previous dream began to repair itself. The autopsies came back for all those who had died after taking his pill, autopsies revealing that other issues were to blame for their deaths. The news crews left his home, and he was being invited to talk shows across the world to talk about the incidents. He was single again, and models from across the world filled up his social media inboxes with pictures and date offers. Life in dream world was good once again. When he woke up, he saw the lunch box on his dresser, then he saw the stack of money on his night stand. He got dressed, grab the lunch box, and headed to the lab to press out 100 pills.

No sooner than he stepped on campus, a girl from his first period class was standing in the middle of the halls handing out black ribbons. She handed one to Josh and explained that a freshman student had died in his sleep the night before. She moved on, handing ribbons to other students as they passed by. Josh looked at the ribbon, confused. He felt uneasy and sad, even though he had no idea who the person was. He could only imagine that this was how other students felt when word got back that he and Lou had been in a deadly car accident. He noticed students huddled in groups in the hallways, no doubt discussing the passing of their peer. Others assisted each other with pinning ribbons to the other's clothing.

It was then he spotted Lance in the distance, heading straight for him. He was walking briskly, moving through the crowd without concern for where anyone stood, he bumped into and pushed many out of his way as he made his way to Josh. Josh could tell something was wrong. Lance asked him for the one hundred pills. Josh held up the lunch box, letting him know he hadn't pressed them out yet. He asked Lance if he knew the kid who died in his sleep. Lance grabbed Josh's arm and ushered him roughly to the nearest restroom.

In the bathroom, he got close in Josh's face and sternly let him know that he had nothing to do with the student dying. Josh was confused, he could read the panic in Lance's eyes. Then, in a moment's time, it became clear that the person who died, had possibly bought a dreamer from Lance.

Josh played it cool. Lance had a bewildered look in his eye, and he didn't want any problems. Lance pushed him up against the wall before storming off. Josh never had a chance to say anything. He just watched Lance's back as he stormed away.

Throughout the day Josh tuned his ears in on conversations about the student whom had died in his sleep. He was seeking information; he couldn't shake the idea that the student's death had something to do with his pills. Now, he was reluctant to create another hundred. He didn't even want to make another one. There was no way to tell exactly how dangerous a withdrawal could become, but he did know that the last time he went to sleep without taking a dreamer, he woke up deeply disturbed. The dreams were too real. By the end of classes that day he had concluded that he wasn't going make any more dreamers, his conscious was torturing him.

He met with Lance at center court of the gym at the end of the day and handed him the lunch box back. Lance opened the box only to find the separated baggies still intact. Josh told Lance that he didn't feel comfortable making the dreamers anymore, that he still needed to do research on the side effects. Lance nodded as if he understood, and together they walked towards the gym's exit. As soon as they stepped outside, Lance grabbed Josh and threw him up against the side of the building, placing the pointy edge of a pocket knife's blade to his throat. He told Josh that he didn't have any choice, either he made the pills, or the side effect of not doing so would be his own death. He shoved the lunch box in Josh's gut. Josh was jolted forward, and the blade pierced his skin, he could feel a trickle of blood running down his neck. Lance put his blade away, popped his collar, and walked off.

Josh knew he had big problems. He hadn't anticipated any of this. He thought back to his original purpose for the experiment, he had only wanted to rest. Oddly enough, he felt more fatigued now than he ever had in his life. At home that night, he battled with taking a dreamer. He was scared to sleep without it, he wasn't sure if you would die or not. Besides that, with all that was going on, he couldn't sleep, his anxiety level was through the roof. He couldn't handle going to sleep and suffering like he had when he hadn't taken the pill two days ago. He only had two dreamers left in his own stash. He vowed that no matter what, when those two were gone he wasn't making anymore dreamers.

In his dream he was attending an award ceremony; he had won a humanitarian award for his great work in the medical field. He was dressed in a black tux and arrived at the event in a Lamborghini. His new girlfriend, an athletic, blonde Olympic volley ball gold medalist hung on his arm. Paparazzi was there, and everyone applauded when he began to walk down the red carpet. He smiled and waved at the crowd as the cameras flashed, celebrities and scholars alike were all lined up to congratulate him on his special day.

Just as the red carpet ended, Lance burst through the crowd, his blade raised high. He swung at Josh. Josh pushed his girlfriend out of harm's way and held up his arm to ward off the blow. The knife came down, slicing his suit and forearm. His security moved in quickly and pummeled Lance to the ground. They dragged Lance away and the event carried on as planned. Josh was credited with saving his girlfriend's life. He even joked about it during his acceptance speech. Then his alarm woke him up.

Josh smiled as he vividly recalled the events of his dream. He wished that he was the same man in real life as he was in his dreams. He knew he was going to miss dreamers. He had one more. Suddenly, he felt a burning sensation on his right forearm. Then his heart filled with dread, he looked down in horror as he saw that his forearm had been sliced open. He quickly grabbed a towel and held it to the wound just as the blood began to drip to the floor.

Josh was scared to leave the house, he had bandaged up his arm and begrudgingly, he got dressed. He stood at the front door of his house for at least seven minutes before he built up the courage to leave. He dreaded running into Lance. He knew that Lance would be looking for the rest of the pills. He was terrified of telling him that he wasn't producing any more. Josh knew that he could miss classes today, but what about the next day, or the day after that? He figured he had to face off with Lance sooner than later, he couldn't hide forever. He only wished he had the same security team that he had in his dreams.

When he got to school, he was beyond nervous. He timidly peered around every corner. He noticed early on that Lance wasn't in the places that he normally was. At mid-day he began to breathe a little easier.

He was buying a candy bar from the vending machine in the commons area when he saw Lance's reflection in the glass behind him. Josh turned around quickly, Lance was wearing shades. Josh could see that Lance had been beaten up. Then he remembered his dream. Nothing and everything was making sense at the exact same time. His forearm was cut, and Lance was beaten up. Lance raised his shades and showed Josh his two black eyes. Then he demanded the pills. Josh realized that Lance was going through withdrawals. He needed the pills, not just to sell, but to feed his own addiction. That is why he was beaten up so badly in his dream. It was his withdrawal. Did their dreams mix? His head pounded from confusion. He told Lance that he was done, that there would be no more pills.

Without hesitation, Lance grabbed Josh's forearm exactly where the laceration was and squeezed tight. Josh grimaced in pain. It took everything in his power not to scream out in agony. He and Lance both knew that what happened in their dreams was shifting into real life. He yanked his arm away and could feel the blood spreading

29

and soiling the fabric of his sleeve.

Lance again demanded the pills, this time pulling out his blade, the tip of it unequivocally sharp. Josh pushed past him and ran, he was sure that Lance had lost all his sanity. He bolted from the common area to the nearest exit and out the building. Lance was in hot pursuit, swinging the knife wildly as he chased, hoping to cut or stab Josh by any means.

Other students looked on in repulsion as the event unfolded. Josh could see them filming the incident on their cell phones, and he wondered if anyone had bothered to call the police. He ran out into the streets, and cars came to a grinding halt, screeching tires. Drivers laid into their car horns, hoping to deter Lance and his blade. None of this dissuaded Lance, he still gave chase as if on a mission. Josh knew that if Lance ever got close enough, he would stab him repeatedly until he died.

He ran towards an apartment building, hoping that at some point Lance would give up. He burst through the apartment buildings double doors, everyone in the lobby screamed as Lance smashed through the door right behind him, his blade flailing through the air. Josh instinctively hit the stairwell and tried to close the door behind him, but Lance burst through, and Josh felt the wind of a missed stab attempt.

Newly motivated, he took the stairs two at a time. Making his way up six flights of stairs before finding himself at the top of the building. He had a gained a slight lead, but now there was nowhere to go. He rushed through the exit door and came out on the roof of the building. The situation was so surreal he wasn't even sure if he was awake or not, this all felt like a horrible dream. He frantically looked for an escape. He could see his entire town from atop the six-story building. He could hear and see the police hurrying for the building. Yet, there was nowhere to go.

Lance came through the door onto the roof, breathing

hard. His shades were gone, and his eyes were blackened and swollen. His face was bruised in several places. Without any thought, he charged at Josh. Josh had no choice but to stand and fight. Lance barreled into Josh and rushed him straight for the edge of the building. The speed and force in which he attacked was too much for Josh to withstand, and before he knew it, they were both soaring over the edge of the building.

Josh's life flashed before his eyes as they fell through the air, waiting to meet the pavement. He asked God for forgiveness and to take care of his mother. It was too late to take anything back; he closed his eyes, and that was the last thing he remembered.

Josh groggily opened his eyes, and then closed them immediately as pain exploded in his cranium. He was scared to open his eyes again, he didn't want to feel the pain. Then, he began to hear muffled conversations. As his ears tuned in, he heard someone say that they had seen him open his eyes. He soon realized that it was the voice of his mother. She sounded excited. So, for her, he opened his eyes again. His head ached, and his vision was slow to adjust. He was in a hospital room, and his mom was hovering over him, her face was only inches from his own. She was crying. Then he saw doctors, and he closed his eyes again.

The doctors raised his bed to an upright position. His mother whispered in his ear that he was going to be ok. She gripped his hand tight. He simply asked, "what happened?"

It took another three days for Josh to be able to communicate effectively with his mother. She told him the story of how Lou had crashed the car doing 90 miles per hour as he sped around a steep curve. How the car left the road and fell in a ditch. How Lou had passed away, and how lucky he was to be alive. None of this made sense to Josh. It was like he had went back in time. He already knew all the things his mother explained. He wanted to know about Lance, and if anyone else had died because of his pills. His mother understood that Josh would be a little disoriented after being in a coma for four days. She listened to him, and her face was flushed with concern. He was speaking about events that never happened.

Josh stayed in the hospital for an additional two weeks. He was having a hard time sleeping, but he was looking forward to being released. When the day of his release came, he sat waiting on the edge of his hospital bed in a paper suit. The doctor came in and told him to take it easy for a while. Take things one day at a time, and eventually, he would be his normal self again. The doctor then handed Josh two pill bottles, one was for pain, and the other was a sleeping aid. Josh took the bottle of sleeping pills and opened them quickly, it was filled with white pills.

He relived the life he had while in a coma. While he knew none of those events had ever happened, they still surged his memory as if they were real occurrences. When the doctor was gone he took the bottle of sleeping pills to the restroom, he knew he wouldn't be needing those. He dumped the pills into the toilet, reached for the handle and flushed. As he watched the pills wash away, amid them all was a single, tiny blue pill.

CAT NAP

The two-story, olive green painted Victorian home sat on the edge of a cul-de-sac. The lawn was spotted with dirt patches, and the hedges weren't groomed. The concrete of the driveway was broken up and worn. There was a one car garage, but there was never a car parked in front of the home. The paint on the face of the house was chipped and splintered, and the shingles were hanging on to their frames haphazardly.

The other four houses that made up the cul-de-sac were well kept. Now, the green house at the end was becoming an eyesore. The children in the neighborhood stepped faster when they passed the house, and it was an urban legend amongst them that the house was haunted. The neighbors used to offer to assist with the lawn care, and one neighbor even volunteered to paint the home free of charge. The people who lived in the olive-green house wouldn't even answer the door most of the time. One time, a neighbor took it upon himself to crank up his riding lawn mower and cut their grass on his own. When he was done with half the lawn, a strapping, pale-skinned woman burst from the house unleashing profanities and throwing canned foods at him. After that, the neighbors gave up. They only hoped that one day the house would be bought, renovated, and become a part of the community.

The neighbors didn't know much about the two women who lived in the green house, except that they were sisters. Patricia and Peggy Lancaster. The most activity anyone had ever seen at the home was an occasional cat in the windows. That was until one of the sisters passed away. The ambulance came blaring, sirens and whirling lights active, in the wee hours of the morning. They loaded Peggy's body onto a gurney, slid her into the back of the ambulance, and drove the body away.

Then there was only Patricia. Patricia was distraught

after her sister passed. She was the only one in her lineage left on the earth. She was no stranger to grieving, though. She and Peggy had almost everything in common. She and her sister were three years apart in age, but lived almost identical lives. They both got married at 20 years old, had two sons and one daughter a piece. Both their husbands died when they were 70, and none of their kids were alive by the time they were 75.

When Patricia's last child passed away, she and Peggy resolved they would live out the remainder of their lives together, in Peggy's home. So that they wouldn't be lonely, they agreed to adopt one cat for each family member that they had lost, totaling eight cats. Within a year, four of those cats had their own litters, and by the end of that same year, they had a total of 22 cats. The sisters were proud of how their family had grown.

Patricia was a diabetic. When she was 77 years old she had lost one of her feet due to diabetes complications. From that point on she was on crutches. Then, it was solely up to Peggy to make the monthly trip to the grocery store to purchase the cat food. Fifty bags of dry, and 200 cans wet.

Peggy was a brawny woman, whereas Patricia was slender and frail. At the beginning of every month Peggy used to pull into the garage with her Crown Victoria weighed down with cat food. It was Peggy who did the bulk of the work, but Patricia would contribute to the best of her ability. It was normally an hour-long job bringing the cat food and other groceries in from the garage to the kitchen. Peggy would always have one of the young men from the grocery to load the food into her car at the store, but the job of unloading the food was left up to the sisters.

Allotting one hour twice a month to make sure their family ate was a minor task to them because they loved the cats almost as much as the actual humans they replaced. They knew all 20 plus cats by name, and they each had their own distinct characteristics. They used to let the cats go and come as they pleased by means of a pet door, but several times some of their cats never came home. So, they had to seal off the pet door. Another year passed, and their family had grown—an additional 13 cats had been born. They were everywhere, there were more cats than furniture. They lounged on the kitchen counters, in the tubs, in the washer and dryer, on and under the beds. One time a cat died, and they couldn't find the body. The house reeked of cat death for weeks until they found the body curled up in the rear of the lower bathroom cupboard. They gave the cat a proper burial in the backyard.

When Peggy passed, it was sudden, and without warning. She never as much as coughed; one day she just didn't wake up. Just like that, Patricia's life was turned upside down. By the time Peggy had passed, they had 43 cats, and Patricia was 81 years old.

Patricia was on her own, and there was no one left to help her. Still, she found comfort with her cats. One month after Peggy's death, the food supply was severely strained. Two weeks after that, there wasn't a cat kibble in the house. When the food for the cats ran out, Patricia unsealed the pet door to let them roam free, in hopes that they could find food for themselves. But some of the cats refused to leave. She shared any food she had left for herself with the cats, and then one day, she was completely out of food. Her cats were starving, they crooned and meowed loudly throughout the day, and more abrasively in the evening. They had begun to eat the couch cushions and all the plants, even the plastic ones. She couldn't get around on her crutches well anymore, so the cat feces had begun to pile up, and the stench was horrendous. Patricia became immune to the smell after a week. She knew she had to try to get out, she had to save her family. She tried one morning and fell as soon as she stepped into the garage. She had to crawl back into the house, and her hip was badly bruised.

What pained her more was the constant crying that

emitted from her cats. She started to notice their weight loss. Some of the smaller cats were being bullied by the bigger cats, and several times she had broken up fights amongst them as best she could with one of her crutches. There were often bite marks on some cats, and various patches of hair strewn about the home. They were doing a lot of biting, and Patricia was concerned that they were now trying to eat each other.

She was down to three cans of beans left in the cupboards. When these three cans were done, she had no idea what she would do for her cats. She had neglected her own health. She had lost twenty-two pounds in the last three weeks. It took all her strength to turn the handle of the can opener. Once that chore was done, she began to pour the cans into three of the 17 food bowls. As soon as the first bean fell into the bowl the cats pounced on the bowls with reckless abandon. The commotion and growls from the pits of their bellies were terrifying and heart-wrenching.

Patricia looked on in dismay, she hated to see her babies suffer. She tried to make sure that they all were able to eat some portion of the beans, and then they turned on her. The clawed and bit at her until she retreated. She was attacked with such ferocity that she couldn't maintain her balance. She fell onto the floor and sobbed, not because she was injured or because the cats nipped at her flesh like piranhas, but because she couldn't stop their suffering.

She wept as she lay on the ground. Then, in her peripheral, she saw the lid from one of the cans of beans laying on the ground beside her. The cats were now on top of her and, biting her face. She could feel trails of blood begin before being quickly licked away by their dry tongues. Patricia gathered what little bit of strength she had left and reached out to grab the jagged tin lid, she held it to her wrist. The cats were suffocating her as they smothered her face, she was almost completely covered by them. She used the jagged edge of the cans lid to slice into her wrist. Her blood began to leak out onto the kitchen floor, and in a few moments, she became light headed. Things weren't so bad now, because she knew her cats would be able to survive for at least another month.

DRILL TIME

"Killing season" was how the month of July was described by the Sun-Times newspaper. Kenyon glanced at the heading of the newspaper while in line at a bodega on South Damen Avenue. He wasn't bothered by the headline, violence was a way of life on the Southside of Chicago. He was only reading to see if anyone in his family had been killed over night.

"Family" is how he referred to the members of his gang, because they were just like family. They needed one another for support and protection. The paper went on to say that four people had been murdered last night. No one from his set had been slain, though. He smiled at that, most of the time he would be able to recognize at least one name on the "body list". Knowing somebody on the list was hit or miss, but it was always guaranteed that there would be a list, daily. He had put some names on the list himself. Several times rival gangs had tried to put him on it. He had been shot in the chest, in the ass, and in the thigh in three separate gun battles over the last 18 months. That was life on the Southside.

Kenyon hadn't asked to be born into this life, but it was the hand given him. The Southside was all he knew, and really, it wasn't that bad. The life of a gangster consisted of parties, drugs, violence, and rest. No other rules to it. His father is a gangster and was locked up with Hoover right now. Kenyon's brother had been murdered only one month earlier, and he was still looking for the person responsible.

At the register, he pulled out a wad of cash and peeled off a ten-dollar bill. He bought a box of cigars and slid them in his pocket. It was 2PM on a Wednesday afternoon, but bullets didn't only fly at night, or on the weekends. So, before he stepped outside the stores doors, he scanned the street outside up and down. Since he carried his pistol so much, he often had to pat his waist section to make sure it was there. He walked outside to the champagne colored Nissan Altima parked at the curb; his girl was waiting for him in the driver's seat. The sun was shining and the afternoon was hot. During the summer, the police department increased their visibility and put extra officers on patrol, because the murder rate was always higher during the warmer months. He casually strolled to the car, opened the door, and fell into the passenger's seat. While she drove, he began to roll some weed. This was how every day began.

The car stereo played a tune from Young Drilla, one of the local rappers in the city who claimed the same gang as him. Kenyon nodded to the heavy bass and chanted the lyrics that related to him personally, names of neighborhoods, names of family members who were still strong in the movement, and the names of fallen soldiers—those who had died in the gang war. His girlfriend reached over and turned the volume down; Kenyon slapped her hand away and turned the sounds back up. He hung his head out the window, looked into the side view mirror, and ran his fingers through his unruly short dreadlocks. With his head out the window he bounced to the music. The average pedestrians and motorist would look at him and quickly divert their attention. It only took a second to recognize what Kenyon represented, and they wanted no problem with the likes of him. If one was to make eye contact, Kenyon would stare at them with a scowl that expressed his defiance to the rules of the land.

The Southside of Chicago had a tense and discouraging feeling about it. A lot of the neighborhood homes were boarded up or vacant from foreclosures. Every business or residence had security bars on the windows and doors. The city train tracks coursed high through the city's buildings, and metro buses moved the city's population throughout the city regularly. Liquor stores, take outs, and beauty supply stores were on most every block. Mixed in with the masses were the Mexican cartel, the GD's, the Black P Stones, and other sets. In fact, on the Southside, there were more gangs and sets than any other city in America. Thugs lurked on the corners hustling single cigarettes or selling drugs, making for a wary atmosphere. The average gang member ranged in age from 14 to 26. The younger the member, the more dangerous they were. Kenyon was 18.

The city had demolished most of the high-rise public housing buildings over the last 10 years, and since then, homicides in the city increased by as much as 50 percent. Largely because gang members in search of new housing often ended up in the wrong neighborhoods, or tried to take over new ones. Huge, empty lots were the remnants of those infamous, low-income housing buildings, but the city had plans for those lots when the rehabilitation began. Whenever that was.

When they passed West Roosevelt road, the gun shots rang out. Not one or two shots, but a repetitious bang that alerted the soul to immediate danger. Instinctively, yet informally, Kenyon ducked low in his seat, his girlfriend dropped her head, barely peering over the steering wheel to see the road ahead. In seconds the gun fire stopped, and they continued to ride normally. Random gunfire was as common as stop signs.

A short while later, she pulled up to a block of houses near Addams Park. There were kids at the park playing, unaware that in some form this alone was Russian roulette. A lot of kids were with their parents. The parents knew that gang violence and shootings materialized more often than the ice cream truck, but they were determined not to be controlled by the thugs who roved the streets. In fact, they even protested on the weekends, meeting in large groups and chanting their disapproval towards the gangs with threats of their own. "We want our neighborhoods back!" they shouted.

The ragged gray house on the end was where several young men sat out on the stoop. There were no telltale signs that these men were gang members, no bandanas. They were shirtless with their pants hanging low; they wore designer belts for show, and still had to manually pull their jeans up by hand most of the time.

Before the car had stopped completely, Kenyon was already out the door and walking to the porch. He set fire to his blunt before he reached his brothers. He slapped hands with them all. They began to talk about who had died the night before, why they died, and who they had planned to kill themselves. Kenyon didn't look back, he only heard his girlfriend pulling away. He couldn't wait to get his Audi back, it was in the shop. Two weeks before he had been in Bronzeville, some Vice Lords wanted to kill him for being there. They shot up his car; his mechanic had counted 78 bullet holes in the Audi. Fortunately for Kenyon, he had only gotten hit in the thigh. He stayed in the hospital overnight and was back on his block within 24 hours, already plotting his retaliation. His set was desperate for revenge, any Vice Lord they saw would die on sight. No matter the time of day or circumstance.

Then there was gunfire.

The men on the porch scrambled to get out the line of fire, tripping over each other while trying to reach the safety of the house, or to get low, where bullets can't fly. Kenyon was pushed passed the corridor and landed inside the house. He could hear the bullets splintering the wooden frame of the house. He heard screams as he lay on the ground, a car's tires as it peeled off and sped away.

Then there was silence.

A silence that had become recognizable to him, the absence of sound in which you can only hear your heart beat, and you know that the next sound you hear would be that of panic. Before he could open his eyes, he heard the shrilling scream of a woman in the distance.

It was then that he realized that he wasn't dead. He sat

up quick and pulled his pistol from his waistband. He looked left and saw his little homey Rod was down, his shirt was drenched in crimson blood, and his body was motionless. He got up and ran outside; he saw two more of his brothers down on the grass, suffering from gunshot wounds, their bodies convulsing in great tremors. Kenyon hopped over them as he ran to the edge of the street, looking up and down it for the car or people responsible for this attack. He could hear the police sirens in the distance. He knew that they would be there in a matter of seconds. He turned and looked back at the bullet riddled house, then down at his fallen comrades. As it stood, his team was losing.

More than 10 people in his gang had been slaughtered in the last month, and even his real blood brother had been murdered. Crying wasn't even a logical emotion. He wanted to run to his car, ride through the hood, and murder anybody who looked like they were claiming a set different from his own. He walked over to JAY-ROC, who was laid out in the grass, his weapon still gripped in his right hand. Kenyon stood over him, and by the way his eyes stared off into oblivion, he knew that JAY-ROC was gone. Kenyon had nowhere to stash his own pistol, so he ran.

The police pulled up in front of the house, screeching tires and hopping out fast just as Kenyon hit the alley. Then the paramedics arrived, then the news crews. In 10 minutes, the entire street was filled with emergency vehicles, a common sight. News crews were notorious for arriving to the scene of a crime even before the police could, mostly because while on site filming one incident, they were likely to hear more gunshots, or get the lead on yet another violent crime only a few blocks away from their initial stories. The news crews on the Southside had plenty to report.

Kenyon darted down an alley alongside the house. He made a quick right down another alley, scaled a fence, and ran another block before coming up behind the back door of his own house. He burst through the door. Although he was the victim of a crime, he still had to flee the scene, because there was never a reason to have to talk to police. Real gangsters hold court in the streets.

When he burst through the door, his oldest brother Lorenz was sitting on the couch in the den. He jumped up quick, snatching his machine gun off of the coffee table. He was a breath away from pulling the trigger when he recognized Kenyon. He could tell by the look on Kenyon's face that he had just been in a gun battle. He had seen that face a million times before.

Kenyon stood in the middle of the den breathing hard and rambling. He vented about revenge, about being tired of losing. When it came to a body count, Kenyon and his set were behind by a large margin. This was a sign of weakness. Lorenz had been a member of the gang since the late eighties. He was 32 now, and he had rubbed shoulders with some gangsters who were legends in their own rights. Upon hearing the news about the murders Kenyon had just witnessed, Lorenz concluded that they must organize a strategic attack to even the score, if not settle it for once and all. Kenyon was all for it, he was ready to run out in the street and just start shooting people, retaliation was a must.

Kenyon calmed down at Lorenz's request and plopped down on the sofa. He shook his head in disbelief, his dreads flailing half hazard. Lorenz lay his machine gun down on the floor and slammed his balled fist into his palm. He consoled his little brother and let him know that a meeting was in order. Somebody would have to pay for what happened, not to mention the death of their real brother. They had to organize, had to make a statement that if any rival chose to violate their set, or pump their nuts up enough to set foot on their turf, they wouldn't leave alive. Kenyon nodded enthusiastically; he couldn't wait to set the tone for a new era. Kenyon knew he had just the tool to assist in this war. He had to pick it up in less than 24 hours and he couldn't wait.

Later that night, they sat around the round table in the basement of the house Kenyon shared with Lorenz. The room was dim and there were 18 people in the crowded quarters. On the small oval table in the center of the basement were a pile of guns. Cigarette and weed smoke wafted through the air, while various bottles of cognac were passed amongst the group. This was a wake of sorts, a time to grieve those who lost their lives for their love of the gang.

Lorenz stood up and braced the table with his palms. He turned his Chicago Bulls snapback ball cap backwards before he addressed the group. At 32 he was the oldest person in the room. The first thing he wanted to know was who didn't have a gun. Out of the 18 people, only four of them were without weapons. They chose from the selection of weapons laid about the table. That order of business taken care of, Lorenz took responsibility for the current loss of lives in his set. He felt he was the blame for not holding this meeting sooner. He was an OG though; when he was Kenyon's age there was organization to war. They would think things through before acting them out. No other set was playing by these old rules, and neither was he, anymore.

His message was that they would rein terror on rival gangs. From now on, they would be the aggressors, and they wouldn't stop until there was total submission. He let the gang know that the war would be long, but history had proven that most turf wars were. While he rallied the members, Kenyon stood posted on a wall, listening to his brother organize what was sure to be one of the bloodiest months the Southside had seen since July. He was amped, he was hoping his brother would say that they were riding out that night, but by the end of the meeting it was decided that the following night would be the first night that they would begin their new wave of vehemence.

Kenyon disagreed with that, he was ready to go, right now! If he had his car, he knew that he and his squad would have already been out looking for rivals. He would have his car out the shop the next afternoon, though.

Kenyon was so eager about getting his car out the shop that he didn't sleep. He was up till 4 am in the basement, reminiscing with his gang about the brothers they had lost. They drank cognac and smoked close to two ounces of weed. The rap music they listened to was inspiring, and graphic enough to fuel the murderous plots they devised. He hadn't told anyone about his car, he knew his friends thought that he was getting some body work and a paint job. They had no idea about the other accessories that he had invested in.

When Kenyon woke up the next day, it was two in the afternoon. He texted his girlfriend and told her he would be ready in 30 minutes. He dressed and groomed himself quickly. No sooner than he had tucked his gun in his waist band, he heard his girlfriend's car horn outside. He ran outside and hopped in the passenger's seat. He cut the radio up and rolled up some weed. He was animated; he hadn't had his car in close to two weeks.

When they arrived, they pulled up to the open doors of the garage and Kenyon hung out the window getting the attention of his mechanic. A dark haired Latino man came from under the hood of a minivan. He wiped his oil-stained hands on a dirty cloth he pulled from his navy blue work pants pockets. Kenyon got out and shook hands with the mechanic, and after getting the word that his car was indeed ready, he waved for his girl to leave.

When she was gone, Kenyon and the mechanic stepped inside the garage. The mechanic let the garage door down and Kenyon followed him through the garage making sure not to get oil on his crisp white sneakers. They crossed through the office; the mechanic picked a clipboard up from off his desk before heading into an adjoining shop.

This shop was as clean as a show room floor. There

were several other cars parked inside, each with a glistening paint job. In the midst of these was his all black Audi. He could only smile when he saw it; the last time he had seen it the front end was mangled, and the entire left side was bullet riddled. Now, it was just as pretty as the day he bought it. It was sleek, with limo tinted windows, black racing rims and racing tires. The car was almost invisible at night, which was perfect for him and his lifestyle. He couldn't wait to whip it around the city again. Everyone would know it was him when he came through. This proved to be a curse and a gift. It was easy for rival gang members to identify him also, the exact reason the car got shot all to hell to begin with. He wasn't worried about that ever happening again.

He walked around the outside of the car, nodding his head in approval. The mechanic read from the clipboard as they circled they car. New paint job? Check! New front end? Check! Bullet proof exterior? Check! Bullet proof windows? Check! They opened the car's driver side door. The mechanic jumped in the driver's seat. He rolled the handle of the turning signal backwards and 90 percent of the dash board folded back, unveiling the ultimate stash spot. Guns, drugs, and excessive amounts of money could be kept here without being discovered during a random traffic stop. Kenyon was super excited. He bounced around the outside of the car like a ten-year-old with a new bike. He had invested a lot into the Audi. He needed a ride as trustworthy as a tank, he was involved in a war. They could shoot at him all they wanted to now, they'd just be wasting their ammo. When the mechanic finally got him to settle down, he showed Kenyon how to adjust the rearview cameras. They couldn't even sneak up on him now, with the rearview cameras; it was like he had eyes behind his head.

Kenyon didn't want or need to hear anymore. He was too eager to ride. He told the mechanic that if he did have any more questions, he would call. Kenyon went in his bulging front pocket and pulled out a fat fold of money. He paid the mechanic his last 3000 dollar cash payment. Kenyon didn't even wait for a receipt, he started the car and it hummed to life. He saw the car's reflection in the mirrors of the garages walls. He liked what he saw. The mechanic met him at the garage door and let the awning up. He watched as Kenyon peeled out the garage, burning rubber before racing up the street, erratic and young. The mechanic shook his head and let down the garage door.

He rode with his pistol on the passenger's seat. He had all the windows down because he wanted to be seen. The car with all its protective amenities made him thirsty for beef. He wished somebody would set trip, they would get more than they bargained for at that exact moment, on sight.

He stopped by his girlfriend's house and picked her up so that they could cruise the city. He didn't care where he rode today, it was his intention to go to every hood, foes or not. He was in a tank. He tried to explain to his girl about everything the car had to offer, but she was only semi-impressed. She respected the game because all her brothers, and even her father claimed a set, but she still thought it was dumb. Her first cousin lost her four-year-old son last year; they were just walking to the store at three in the afternoon when it went down. Every time she thought about how tore up her cousin was at the funeral, she wanted to cry. She told Kenyon that when their child was born they had to leave the Southside; she didn't want to experience what her cousin had. Kenyon had told her that she would be leaving by herself, because he loved his hood. He was dumb. She felt a little better knowing that the car was bullet proof, but she didn't want to find out if it worked or not. She could tell that Kenyon was itching to find out, so she asked to be dropped off at her girlfriend's house after only 30 minutes of riding.

Kenyon dropped her off and headed to his house, he couldn't wait for his brother to see the Audi now. It had been resurrected. When he pulled up in the driveway, he called his brother on his cell phone and told him to come outside. A moment later Lorenz came from the house, shirtless. Before he made it to the car he was already nodding and grinning. Lorenz got in the passenger's side, and Kenyon wasted no time running down the commodities of the vehicle. When he flipped the turn signal in reverse and the stash box was revealed, Lorenz was impressed. He pulled a .380 handgun from his pocket and tossed it in the box. Kenyon closed the box and Lorenz nodded in approval. He couldn't even tell that the dash was removable. Kenyon told him about the bullet proof exterior, and Lorenz knew that he would be riding with his little brother tonight. They took a moment to roll up the windows and smoke some trees. Then they headed inside, it would be dark in two hours, and it would be time to ride.

It was 11 at night when Kenyon, Lorenz, and two other gangsters loaded themselves into the Audi. There was no need to put their guns in the stash box, not only were there too many, but they would be using them. They rode with guns in their laps and laying on the floor board of the car. Between the four occupants there were a total of eight guns, two apiece. Six hand guns and two assault rifles. Their entire motorcade was made up of three vehicles. They were four-deep in every car, and not a single person wasn't strapped with a weapon. Kenyon whipped through the streets feeling invincible, he knew that he had a one up in this war, not only the element of surprise, but his investment of turning his vehicle into a war machine.

When they were two blocks away from their rival's blocks. Kenyon cut the radio down. The crew loaded and cocked their weapons. Kenyon was ready. The memory of his deceased brother and friends powered his motivation for revenge. He slapped hands with Lorenz and looked in his rear view, the other members of his motorcade drove past and around, stationing themselves in various locations throughout the neighborhood, virtually surrounding it. When the bullets began to fly, no matter where they would run, they would run into Kenyon and his gang.

Moments later Lorenz phone rang, he had the word that everyone was in position and ready. Kenyon started the car and made the first right into the neighborhood. At the top of the block they could see a group of gangsters mingling on the corner with no cares, they were in their own hood, where it was safe. Kenyon couldn't wait to upset their sanctuary.

He drove slowly and pulled up directly in front of a group of about seven men standing in front of the corner store. Then Kenyon let the windows down, and all the occupants aimed their weapons. The men in front of the store knew what was next as the recognition of what was happening unfolded. Almost simultaneously, everyone pulled out their guns.

Kenyon and his squad had a moment jump on the situation and they fired first. Kenyon and his men fired into the crowd maliciously, chopping bodies down like trees. Some were able to return fire, but their bullets bounced off the body of the Audi. They exchanged gun fire for almost eight seconds, yet, it felt like an hour. There was screaming and the stringent scent of gun powder. Even when Kenyon and his men fell back into the vehicle, he could still here gunfire. Kenyon smiled as he let up the windows, knowing that his gang was terrifying the hood at other ends.

Unexpectedly, the Audi jolted violently as it was rammed in the back. The hit had damaged his rearview cameras and he couldn't see who was behind him. Then, the Audi began to rock like a boat as bullets pummeled the vehicle. He hit the gas, peeling off. His investment was paying off, as no one in his car had not been hit by a bullet. At half a block, without warning, a SUV with a bulky grill guard barreled into the passenger's side door of the car, crashing the Audi into a telephone pole, the Audi stalled out now trapped between the SUV and the pole.

Kenyon and his men began to panic slightly. The car was being riddled by bullets and although they couldn't penetrate the car, the consistency by which they were bombarded was frightening. Lorenz yelled for Kenyon to pull off, he could see they were being surrounded and outnumbered. Kenyon pressed the gas and the engine raced loudly, but the car would not move. The gang encircled the Audi, but Kenyon felt confident knowing they would run out of ammo before any of their bullets could hurt anyone inside. He assumed the gang would have to retreat soon as he heard police sirens wailing in the distance, then they could take their chances on foot.

As the men reached the vehicle Kenyon threw up his middle finger, laughing in the gunmen's faces as they tried to get in. Instinctively Kenyon put the Audi in park, so that he could throw up gang signs at the men through the glass. He never had a chance to twist up his fingers, for he recognized his mistake. When he put the vehicle in park, the doors automatically unlocked themselves.

THE CHALLENGE

12 p.m.

Thomas Andrews sat at his computer as he finished his BLT on rye, taking a moment to stare out his office window at the snowy knolls of Utah. In January this was a beautiful sight. He crumpled the wax paper his sandwich had been wrapped in and shot it into the waste basket near his feet. He looked to his computer to do a final review of all the events leading up to the space shuttle Champion launch. Thomas was just as excited as the rest of the country about the launch, but as an engineer for Norton and Thickle, he had even more reason to be exuberant about it. Norton and Thickle had secured the contract to construct the rocket boosters that would catapult the space shuttle Champion into space. Thomas would brag to just about anyone about his job and their contract with NASA. Besides, it wasn't every day that you would run into a rocket scientist.

The Champion shuttle launch was big news, the President of the United States was set to rave about the space shuttle at the State of the Union Address the very same evening of its launch. The launch of the Champion had been one of the biggest topics in the news for the past year, and Thomas was elated to be a part of such a grand juncture. Every so often, he would take a moment to view the Cape Canaveral event log as NASA prepared. Everything was looking officially superb. Thomas leaned back in his office chair and stretched. In mid-stretch his brow twitched, and he leaned in close to the computer. He noticed something, something small enough to be overlooked, but significant enough to be disastrous. He picked up his desk phone and called Robert, another engineer who worked closely with him on most projects. "Can you come in my office really quick," Thomas asked, when Robert answered.

Robert came into the office almost as soon as he placed the receiver back in its cradle.

"What's the good word?" Robert asked, entering the office holding a bag of chips. He was just as jovial about the launch as Thomas.

"Come here and look at this," Thomas said.

Robert could tell by the stern look on Thomas face that something was wrong. "What you got?" he asked as he rounded the desk to look at the computer. Robert stared at the event log on Thomas's computer for extended seconds before looking to Thomas. "What?" he finally asked perplexed.

"Look at the temperature tomorrow," he replied.

Robert looked at the screen again, eating a hand full of chips while he read. It only took a moment before he understood the urgency and disdain in Thomas facial expression. The temperature forecasted in Cape Canaveral at the time the space shuttle was supposed to launch was predicted to be unusually low, a record breaking 30 degrees Fahrenheit. This would be the coldest morning ever for a launch to take place. "Oh my God, that's not good," Robert said out loud. More to himself than to Thomas. "We need to take this to management," he concluded before balling up the now empty bag.

Thomas agreed.

In a few short moments after Thomas's discovery, the hallways of Norton and Thickle aerospace corporation were filled with engineers. The concern was great, seven of the 10 engineers assigned to the project had gathered to take their findings to the Vice President. They had major apprehensions about the launch, and they had taken it upon themselves to take the situation to management. Lives were at stake. Thomas was the first to burst into the Vice President's office. The man looked up from his paperwork as his office filled with engineers. He snatched off his glasses. "What the hell is going on here?" he asked.

Thomas marched up to the desk and unfolded the

blueprints that he was carrying atop it. "The temperatures at tomorrow's launch are too low. We can't launch the shuttle if the temperatures don't warm up," Thomas said up front.

The Vice President stared at the prints rolled out on his desk then back up at Thomas. "What are you talking about?" he said finally.

"The launch tomorrow, "Robert chimed in. "The seals will not hold with the temperature being so low, its predicted to be only 30 degrees Fahrenheit at the time of launch. We certainly have to wait until a warmer day to launch."

The Vice President chuckled a little and looked around at the room full of engineers. "So, your telling me to call NASA and stop the launch because it's going to be too cold," he said, facetiously.

"That's exactly what we're saying!" Thomas said, empathically.

6 p.m.

Thomas, Robert, and 8 other engineers all met in the dimly lit conference room to present their case to the President of Norton and Thickle. The V.P. was in attendance with two other top management officials. They all sat around the 18-foot dark walnut executive conference table their eyes affixed on Thomas who stood in front of the room at the projector. "The temperature will be 30 degrees at launch tomorrow," Thomas began. He placed a film on the projector, the projector cast a diagram of the booster seals that held the rockets together onto the projector screens.

"Everyone in this room knows that when a shuttle takes off, great energy works the joints of the boosters and creates disruptive forces that make some of the seals act faulty. More importantly, the colder the temperature, the faultier the seals become." Thomas removed the film and placed another film on the projector. This film detailed the findings from the previous test launches. He presented film after film on the slide for near 30 minutes before he was done with his presentation. Thomas had already known that he had the support of the other engineers in the room, he just had to get the higher officials on board—which he thought would be relatively easy after his presentation.

When Thomas was done the room was quiet. The President sat staring at the projectors screen, tapping his pen on the wood of the conference table. After a few seconds, he finally spoke, "So, if the shuttle launches tomorrow with temperatures being as low as forecasted, there is a good possibility that, what? What's the worst-case scenario?"

Robert spoke up, "It's not an if sir. The shuttle will blow up."

The room became deathly quiet. The President took a moment to look at the faces of all the engineers in the room. They were all solemn. They were unified, it was imperative that the launch be delayed until a warmer day. It was a life or death situation.

The President looked to the V.P. "Get NASA on the phone and set up a meeting to discuss these issues before the night ends," he said.

8 p.m.

Thomas, Robert, eight other engineers, four top managers, the President and Vice President of Norton and Thickle met in the conference room for a second time. Only this time, there was an office phone in the middle of the oblong table.

From his seat, Thomas stared at the telephone as the President punched in the numbers to NASA's Marshal Committee at the space flight center. After two rings a strong, commanding voice answered on the other end of the speakerphone. The group of engineers and management officials listened in as the President chatted with one of Nasa's top officials, giving him a briefing as to the gravity of the call.

"Tell me what you got," the voice crackled through the phones small speaker.

The President nodded at Thomas and slide the base of the phone in Thomas direction.

Thomas leaned close to the phones mic. "Marshall, we have four viable issues with tomorrow's launch," Thomas began. He hadn't expected to be nervous talking to a phone, but he was just as nervous as he would have been if had been talking to the officials face to face. He cleared his throat before he continued. "For several years it has been noted that during takeoff inordinate forces tend to cause the seals where the rockets fit together not to hold as securely as we would like them to. We have also determined over the last few years that the colder the weather, the harder it is for the booster seals to stay engaged with the rockets. Just last year, for instance, as you well know Marshall, NASA launched a shuttle at 53 degrees Fahrenheit, the coldest it has been thus far for a launch, and nearly half the booster seals on the rocket were damaged because of it. Our research has consistently affirmed that at 50 degrees Fahrenheit or lower, the booster seals will most certainly fail. We have compiled detailed evidence to promote our findings. Tomorrow, the launch is scheduled to take place at 30 degrees Fahrenheit." Thomas looked around the table at the faces of his comrades for confirmation that he wasn't forgetting anything. Robert gave him the thumbs up, and Thomas leaned back in his chair.

There was a long silence on the line. Everyone in the conference room could hear as two NASA Marshalls chatted amongst themselves before one of them finally said, "So, what's the final consensus?"

Thomas looked to the President and Vice President for authorization to answer. They nodded, giving him the go-ahead.

Thomas took a deep breath, leaned in towards the speaker phone and said, "It is imperative that the launch not ensue at its scheduled time, unless we see warmer temperatures in Cape Canaveral."

There was a moment of silence, then a voice boomed over the speaker. "Are you guys over there serious?! What do you mean that we can't launch tomorrow?! The entire world, including the President of the god damn United States are anticipating the Champion's launch tomorrow! You guys are telling us that less than 24 hours before we go to space, we are supposed to just halt progress based on the temperature! My God! Did we contract with the right company on this or not!?"

The President and the Vice President of Norton and Thickle looked at each other in horror. They hadn't expected such dramatic backlash from NASA. They were only trying to be transparent and safe.

"Give us a moment to review some things Marshall," The President said nervously into the speaker before putting the NASA officials on mute.

8:30 p.m.

The President got up and walked to the head of the table. He braced both edges of it before he spoke. "Are you guys sure that there is no way we can get this thing off the ground," he said to the room.

All the engineers shook their heads no empathically. They were all certain that a launch at 30-degree temperatures would be fatal for the astronauts.

The President stood erect. "All right, here's what we will do," he began. "Anyone who's in favor of going ahead with the launch, raise your hand."

Not a single hand in the room went up.

Robert spoke up. "If we approve this launch, we will all be back in this conference room for a much graver reason."

"You absolutely can't launch tomorrow," Thomas added. "The damn thing will blow up!" he yelled slamming his fist on the conference table.

The President took a moment to process the situation.

He stared at the phone where he knew NASA Marshalls were not only waiting, but waiting for the go-ahead. Anything else, he knew, would not be acceptable. Not only was the Norton and Thickle reputation on the line, but their entire contract with NASA.

"You know what," the President began as he paced the room. "Since we cannot come to an agreement, management themselves will make the final call on this."

He looked to the Vice President and the other four senior managers in the room. "I vote yes," the President said.

The Vice President dropped his head. "I vote yes too," he said lowly, never looking up from the table.

Thomas looked around the room. The other engineer's eyes were bulging from shock.

Then, another senior manager agreed, as well as two others. The final senior manager did not agree, he simply got up and left the room.

"Well its official!" The President said triumphantly! "We are moving forward as planned!"

"You can't!" Thomas said standing up swiftly. "It's not safe. It will blow up!" He implored.

The President shot Thomas an angry glare with his finger on the mute button of the phone. He didn't have to say anything more to Thomas. Thomas read his expression and sat down. His heart was beating fast, and he felt a burning behind his pupils. He wanted to cry.

8:45 p.m.

The President pressed the mute button on the phones speaker. "We have reached an agreement," he said into the speaker, never taking his eyes off Thomas.

"What you got?" the voice crackled from over the line.

"We have unanimously agreed that we are going to move forward as planned. We look forward to a successful launch tomorrow," he announced.

The entire conference room was subdued. The President of Norton and Thickle had just condemned innocent human beings to a death sentence.

"That's what we like to hear," one of the Marshalls said. "Get the paperwork here via fax immediately." Then the phone line went dead.

Thomas stood and hurriedly left the conference room. He bolted down the hall to the bathroom and burst through the door and hit the stall just in time to vomit into the commode.

Thomas left the building that evening completely unsettled. He couldn't believe what was happening. He almost wanted to call the police, the governor, someone, anyone. He drove home in a fog, he swerved while he drove as if he had been drinking. When he finally pulled into the driveway of his ranch style home, he didn't understand how he had made it. He got out of his car and stumbled into the house. When his wife saw him, she ran to him from the den and caught him before he collapsed. She began to cry at just the sight of him. "Honey! What happened, are you ok!?" she exclaimed. He looked as if he had been drinking and fighting.

He put a great portion of his body weight on her as he limped to the couch and fell into its cushions. Once he was stable, his wife went to the restroom and returned with a cold rag for his forehead.

"Thomas, tell me what's going on?" she said sympathetically as he placed the rag on his forehead.

He took a moment to gather himself. "The space shuttle Champion," he said through labored breaths. He was almost hyperventilating. "It's going to blow up," he said before he started to weep.

His wife pulled him close and rocked him like a baby. She was concerned. "What do you mean blow up?" she asked, after a moment.

After a few seconds, he composed himself and looked her in the eye. "The shuttle will blow up tomorrow," he said, frankly.

Later that evening Thomas and his wife sat on the

front porch swing bundled up under a blanket together and sipping hot tea. They both viewed the starry heavens in silence as they swung. Thomas had already briefed her on his findings and his expectations. She tried to be optimistic, her only consolation was that he had done all that he could do. Thomas wasn't so sure.

Thomas only slept for 17 minutes the entire night. He didn't eat or drink coffee that morning as he dressed and begrudgingly left for work. In fact, that sandwich on rye the afternoon before was the last time he'd eaten anything. He had no appetite. When he got to work, he saw Robert in the parking lot. His eyes were bloodshot red, and he had puffy bags under them. Thomas knew that he hadn't slept either. They walked into the offices of Norton and Thickle together; neither said anything to the other.

Inside, no one in the office had much to say as they waited for the moment when the space shuttle Champion would launch. It had been a grand ordeal up until just 24 hours earlier, what they had all looked forward to the past year was now what they all dreaded. They piled into the exact conference room where they had spoken with NASA just 12 hours earlier. The projector screen was already showing live footage from Cape Canaveral Florida. The astronauts crossed the tarmac in route for the Shuttle, helmets in hand, waving to family and friends as they one by one boarded the shuttle. The entire nation was engaged, across the country, parents, teachers, children and others gathered in front of their television screens. Everyone waiting in expectation of a grand event, except for the 40 employees of Norton and Thickle. They were watching the exact same events as the rest of the world, except, instead of euphoria, they watched with fear and dread in their hearts.

When the last astronaut donned his helmet and boarded the shuttle, Thomas began to feel light headed. He stood up; he couldn't sit any longer. They all listened as the entire United States counted down together. 10, 9, 8....

At the count of 1, a great fire erupted from underneath the shuttle as the rockets ignited and lifted the shuttle for the heavens at 2000 miles per hour.

The engineers watched with crossed fingers and prayers in their hearts for all the souls aboard. Then, after the shuttle had been in the sky for one minute. Robert stood up, "By God, I think we're going to be ok," he said.

There was a sigh of relief throughout the room, and it was then that Thomas realized that he hadn't taken a breath since the one count. Thirteen seconds after that, the space shuttle Champion burst into flames killing everyone on board.

LUTHOR VS CLARK

Luthor had been the most popular person on campus since his very first day of high school. The summer before his freshman year began, he had grown into his looks. He had a strong square jaw and was all muscle. He had run two miles a day for the entire summer, and it showed. He was ripped. His physical features were only a bonus to all the other benefits of being Luthor. He was born into wealth, his parents were both prolific politicians, recognized and respected throughout the metropolis.

On the first day of high school, he pulled up to the front doors and hopped out of his stealth, metallic black, brand new droptop 5.0 Mustang. Everyone saw him, and everyone was in awe. It wasn't because of the awesomeness of the mustang 5.0, but because he wasn't even of driving age. His butler got out on the passenger's side and walked around to open the driver's side door to let Luthor out. Luthor was dressed modestly in just a t-shirt and jeans. His t-shirt highlighted his physique, his chest, arms and back well defined.

As he headed up the stairs for the double doors of the high school, all the girls clutched their books to their chests, their eyes glazed over. Never in the high school's entire existence had a freshman been so coveted by the girls, even the seniors. That first day set the tone for the first three years of his high school experience. He was the most popular guy in the school, and he reigned uncontested until his senior year. It was then that things began to change.

Luthor had certainly been the ladies' man, and the most popular guy in the building since the first day of school. He had dated every popular girl that walked the campus, most times it was the most two popular girls, at the same time. He never had just one girlfriend, the thing was, he never gave one girl the tittle of girlfriend. Most of the time they were ok with that, he had that much charisma. He had that much money. He had that much power. There was a dark side to Luthor, though. None of the girls he had dated ever spoke much about that side, but they all knew it, or had experienced it. It was almost like he would hypnotize them into submission.

There was one girl named Sal, she had told her two best friends about what a douchebag Luthor was. She told them that he was way too aggressive, that he had bruised her wrist while holding her down, attempting to have his way with her. She even showed them the bruises. Sal's friends told her that she had to tell the principal about the incident. Sal was hesitant at first, but after some coercing, she finally agreed that Luthor had to pay. She and her two friends marched into the principal's office the very next day, and while Sal cried and told the principal about her awful experience in the back of Luthor's Jaguar, her friends stood behind her as moral support. By the time Sal was done, all three girls were in tears.

When the tears slowed, the principal simply asked, "Why were you in the back of his Jaguar?"

The faces of the three girls dropped to the shiny tiled floors. The principal didn't even wait for a reply. He simply sent them on their way. They couldn't move, shock had cemented their feet to the floor. The principal got up from behind his desk and physically shooed them towards the door, he slammed it when they were on the other side. The parents of all three girls removed them from the school the next day. Luthor was invincible, he did what he wanted. His parents virtually owned the city, to challenge him only meant that you wanted to make you existence in that city volatile. That all changed when Clark started at the high school during Luthor's senior year.

When Clark showed up, Luthor was immediately aware that now, finally, he had competition. Clark was athletic and charismatic, even the glasses he wore made him more intriguing. The girls at the school always talked about his sleek black hair and his soft-spoken demeanor. Clark was in sharp contrast with Luthor, as far as personality goes. Whereas Luthor was obnoxious and vocal, Clark was quiet and secluded. By the middle of the school year, Clark had just as many admirers as Luthor. Thing was, Clark never dated any of them. Clark didn't have a car and appeared to be almost poor. He was fast though, Clark was the fastest track competitor in the state.

Clark's presence at the school didn't change Luthor. Clark was not the threat he thought he would have been. Luthor didn't mind sharing his popularity with the girls with Clark, mostly because Clark wasn't giving any of them the time of day, Clark was more into his studies. That all changed one Saturday night.

Luthor was on a date with a freshman named Liza. They had drove to make-out mountain in his sport edition Wrangler Jeep with the removable top. They drove up the small mountain and parked at Lovers Cliff, an edge of the mountain where you could park and view the city skyline in all its splendor, without ever leaving the vehicle. They had ended up in the back seat rather quickly. Luthor had been eagerly anticipating getting her to the mountain, so he didn't bother to take the top off the jeep. He needed the privacy. Liza was a freshman, but she was built like a senior. Only ten minutes after they had parked, he had already made it to second base with her. He reached to unbutton her jeans, and she grasped his hand and said, "No."

There was something about the word that Luthor despised, probably because he never heard it, except sometimes from girls when he was swinging for the homerun. Luthor continued his advances and Liza grew frightened. She dug her nails into his hand to get his attention. Luthor saw red, he reared back to punch her in the face. He thought better of that, he didn't want to bruise her face, so he choked her. Luthor wasn't a rapist, there were plenty of girls in the city willing to have sex with him, but he did have an issue with being told no. He especially didn't like to be fought. This wasn't about the sex anymore, this was about respect. He applied a little pressure to his grip, just so she would understand who she was dealing with.

Then, without warning, the entire top of his jeep was removed, peeled off like a can of sardines. In an instant, Luthor was being pulled up out his jeep by his lapel. Luthor only had a moment to turn to see who had appeared, as if out of the sky's, while possessing the strength of 10 men. Luthor's bladder released as he was tossed to the ground as easy as a stuffed animal. He landed harshly in the gravel on his face, his nose and mouth filling with dirt and bits of rock. He rolled over quickly and saw Clark lifting his date from the car. Luthor's instinct was to get up and fight, but he was too weak. The magnitude of the event was too abnormal. So, he sat in the dirt watching as Clark and his date disappeared into the darkness.

Luthor drove home roofless. Every so often he would look up into the open sky almost expecting to see Clark standing over him. His fists clenched the steering wheel tight as he relived the embarrassment Clark had caused him. Every so often, he would look into the rearview mirror at his reflection. The gravel had left a series of deep scratches on the left side of his face, beginning at the top of his lip and ending at the base of his ear. No one had ever challenged him in such domineering fashion! Where did he come from!? Was he followed!? It was highly unlikely that Clark would randomly be on make-out mountain. He never dated. Who did he think he was ripping the roof of his car off like that?! How could he rip the roof off his Jeep like that?!

Luthor looked at the latches that would have normally held the removable top in place, they were bent. Clark was the fastest guy in the state, and now Luthor understood why, it was obvious. Clark was on steroids! By the time pulled he pulled onto the winding driveway of his parents' mansion, he vowed that Clark would have to pay for what he had done. He knew he had to level the playing field.

The next day at school Luthor saw Clark in the hallway, by himself like always. Luthor stared at Clark hard, trying to get a reaction. Clark never even looked his way. Clark was so unbothered that for a moment, Luthor even began to second guess if it had been Clark who had ripped off his roof and tossed him to the earth like a rag doll. It wasn't until he saw Liza in the cafeteria that afternoon that he knew for sure. Liza and her friends snubbed him. That was a first. He had been on a million dates, some had ended worse than the last, but never had he been snubbed.

The fury that welled in his chest was like none that he had ever felt before. Luthor left the cafeteria for the gym in a blind fury. In the gym he headed for the locker rooms. He went down a line of lockers punching dents into each one as he passed. He wanted revenge. His fist throbbed with pain after punching the sixth locker. He sat down on a bench in the locker room, his chest was heaving, and he knew there was no time to waste.

After school he drove straight to the family doctor who had been his since birth.

His doctor peered at him from across his desk. "Steroids?" he asked incredulously.

Luthor was firm in his request. The doctor was hesitant. He knew that it would be inappropriate to supply Luthor with the drug, it was dangerous. "Did you get approval from your parents?" the doctor asked.

Luthor was infuriated. He didn't like to be questioned or played for the dummy. In a swift motion, Luthor was up and over the desk with a fist full of the doctor's lab coat balled up in his hand. The frail doctor was almost pulled out of his seat. "Of course, I have my parent's approval," Luthor snarled into the doctor's face.

The doctor threw up his hands. "Ok, Luthor," he said.

Luthor pushed the doctor back into his office chair.

The doctor adjusted his jacket and pulled a small pad from his office desk. He took a pen from his lab jacket pocket and scribbled out a prescription for steroids on a pad. He ripped the prescription from the pad and slid it across the table at Luthor. Luthor regained his composure and picked up the prescription. He folded it neatly and put it in his pocket before leaving the doctor's office. The doctor stared at the closed door shaking his head. "Just like his father," he mumbled to himself.

Months passed and the damage was irreversible. Gone was the charismatic charm that had used to work on the girls. Since the incident with Liza, the girls now shunned him. There was a rumor in the school that Clark had saved Liza from being raped. That was a lie, he had never raped anyone! What was more infuriating was that Clark still walked around as if nothing had happened. Not once, in an entire three months' time, had Clark even so much as glanced in his direction. The audacity!

Luthor had trained hard in the gym. With the aid of the steroids he was taking, he could feel his power growing. After 60 days, he could see his body changing, his biceps began to bulge, his trapezoids swelled, and his legs began to resemble tree trunks.

One day, after a workout, he stood in the gyms mirror staring at the transformation. He began to laugh hysterically after a few moments. Not at his appearance, that was a work of art in itself. He laughed because as the months had passed, no one had the slightest idea as to what he had been planning. Not Liza, and especially not Clark. They had really believed that the incident at make-out mountain had passed without consequence. As if he wasn't Luthor.

Then, the day arrived when he would exact his revenge. He wanted the entire school to witness this day. There was a pep rally for the basketball team in the Gym. The entire school was crowded into the gym for the rally. The band engaged the crowd with triumphant drums, horns, and symbols. Luthor wanted to make a dramatic entrance so he stood outside of the gym's double doors. Waiting for his moment. When he heard the band stop playing, and the basketball coach start to speak through the bullhorn, Luthor took a step back and with great force he kicked the gym doors open. The doors flew open violently and the crowd all hushed at once. Luthor crossed the gym floor wearing only a A-frame t-shirt and cargo shorts. He wore wrestling boots tied up tight to the knee, and he had been sure to take an extra dose of steroids before the moment.

Luthor crossed the gym floor more confident than he had ever been in his life. He had been waiting for this moment. While the entire school thought that he had just disappeared into the realms of the normal, today he would show them that he was far from normal. He was exceptional, he was dominant, he was Luthor.

He snatched the bullhorn from the basketball coach and pushed him down to the floor with great force. The schools only security guard was standing close by and before Luthor could raise the bullhorn the security guard had grabbed his free arm. Luthor bought the butt of the bullhorn down hard on the head of the guard, crumpling him to the floor. The crowd gasped and several people screamed.

"CLARK!!!!!!" Luthor yelled into the bullhorn. The mania in his voice was undeniable. Students began to bolt for the exits. They were witnessing a man gone mad. The gym began to clear as students stampeded for the doors. It took less than 30 seconds for sixty percent of the gym to clear. Luthor didn't care, he was only focused on finding one person. Then he saw him. Clark was sitting in the middle of the bleachers. All those around him had dispersed, and he still sat there, undeterred. This infuriated Luthor beyond measure. The audacity!

Luthor saw red; he rushed the bleachers, taking them two at a time. When he was only feet from Clark, he threw the bull horn at his face and leaped into the air with his arm reared back, hoping to land a lethal blow. Clark was extremely fast, never getting up, he slid to the side and watched as Luthor crashed into the bleachers. A teacher screamed. Luthor was back on his feet in an instance. He took a swing at Clark who was still sitting. Clark dodged that blow, and as Luthor followed up with another he caught his fist and held it in his grip. He applied pressure and Luthor's brow folded in. His face turned blush red. Luthor knew that Clark could crush his entire hand if chose to, his strength was super human. The realization that he had bit off more than he could chew registered at that moment. Clark was some type of freak. Clark let Luthor's hand go and stood up. He headed for the gyms exit while Luthor stared at his mangled hand in horror. His hand throbbed with pain. It was beet red, and he couldn't un-ball his fist.

Luthor watched as Clark left the gym nonchalantly. Although in pain, his mind was already plotting his revenge. Steroids weren't enough. He had to take greater measures now. He had witnessed things others hadn't with Clark, he knew that Clark was different. He determined that he would figure out how different Clark was. But, he wouldn't stop there, he would ultimately want to hurt him as much as Clarke had hurt and embarrassed him.

Luthor stumbled for the gym's exit holding his maimed hand with his good one.

As soon as he exited the gym's doors, the police were already waiting for him with their guns drawn. They yelled for Luthor to put his hands in the sky. He couldn't, his right hand was damaged severely. The coppers assumed Luthor was being defiant, just as was reported during the initial call in. So they fired a shot, hitting the brick of the school behind him. Luthor dropped to his knees and the cops moved in swiftly, yanking his hands behind his back with no regard for his injury. Luther howled in pain. He blamed Clark. His life had been everything he expected till this freak of nature showed up.

Luthor was tossed into the back of a police cruiser, his hand near crushed. All the students who had ran from the gym stood outside the school watching as Luthor sat in the rear of the police car, sweating with his teeth clenched from the unbearable pain surging through his hand. What pained him more was watching all his classmates stare as he was carted off for jail. The same faces that had admired him for the last four years. As the police cruiser began to move, he saw Liza in the crowd. She waved goodbye, and for that instant, Luthor forgot about the pain in his hand. The adrenaline, and thirst for revenge that surged through his veins was more potent. He didn't know who Clark was, or where he came from, but he did know that Clark wasn't prepared for the war that he had just inherited, he didn't care who, but one of them would die.

LACEY

I met her at a house party when I was 15. I still remember that night because it changed my life. I didn't dance much that evening. I just sat around with a few friends listening to music. We were entertained by the young ladies who re-enacted mature dance moves. There was one girl who I saw dancing with a lot of people. She would spend a moment with them and then move on.

The first couple of times she passed me I didn't say anything. Still, I kept bumping into her throughout the night. My friend Jay finally introduced us. Her name was Lacey, and she was from California. She was very attractive, one of the prettiest girls I'd ever met. She was quiet during the introduction, but her perfume spoke volumes. The fragrance she wore was bold and intoxicating.

Finally, Jay left her and me alone to get to know each other. I can still remember our first kiss. How it happened is still vague. Maybe it was the music, the lighting, or just because it was a party. There was nothing that led up to the kiss; it was an unspoken agreement. The first kiss was brief, and then a longer more passionate kiss followed. Her perfume was seductive and her lips were addictive. When the kiss was over, she started to dance for me. I sank deep into my chair and relaxed. By the way that she moved I knew that she liked me, and before the evening ended, she was my girlfriend.

From that night forward, I and Lacey were inseparable. We went to school together, ate lunch together, and sometimes after school she would come over to my house. There were a few times that I'd sneak her into my room and let her spend the night. I hid my relationship with her from my parents because, subconsciously, I knew they wouldn't approve of her. She was a distraction, and because I was in love, I was blind to a lot of things. I spent so much time with her that I was never inspired to do anything other than be with her.

One evening I got caught. Lacey was spending the night when my parents came home from their movie earlier than I thought. They caught the two of us in my room. My mom was livid. She went on about how she knew Lacey's type, and how she was much too fast for me. She said she was no good and was never allowed over again. I apologized, then Lacey and I left. Outside, I kissed her one last time and told her that I'd see her the next day.

That night, my father sat me down in the living room and told me about how he once dated a girl just like Lacey. He understood where I was coming from. He said that it wasn't until he met my mother that he broke the relationship off. He told me to be careful, to make sure I was always in control of the relationship, and to never let her control me.

I continued dating Lacey. I couldn't help it, she made me feel good. When I was feeling down, she brought me up. It got to the point that nothing was entertaining unless she was with me. We watched movies and even studied. Whatever I did, I enjoyed it more with her. She became my steady woman throughout high school.

Three months after graduation I moved out. I was unsure about going to college, so I discussed this with Lacey. She told me that I had plenty of time to go to school in the future. For the moment, she wanted it to be just her and me.

So, I got a job at a warehouse. Sometimes Lacey would show up for my lunch break. When I got home, she would be waiting for me arms open wide. On the weekends we'd go out, and we never had a bad time.

Everything was good for a long time, but supporting us was draining my bank roll. To make matters worse, I eventually lost my job. There were many nights that I stayed up late with her, and the next morning, I wouldn't have the motivation to go to work. Or, some mornings I would roll over and see her looking lovely as always, we would kiss, and after that, I knew I wouldn't be going anywhere.

The day I lost my job I came home to my small apartment and told Lacey what had happened. We thought about what would be best for us for almost two hours before she came up with a solution. It was an idea that only a true lover would conceive, much less commit to. She wanted to help me out so desperately, that she volunteered to prostitute herself. I was taken aback by her proposal, and at first, I didn't think I had it in me to share her with others. We talked about it all night, and by morning, we had come to the conclusion that we were going to do it.

The first thing I did was consult with my old high school crony Jay. I told him my plans. I wanted him to help me get the business off the ground. It didn't take long for word to travel, and pretty soon, Lacey and I were as busy as ever. We would sit in the apartment and wait for clients to knock on the door; they would pay for her services and leave. She must have been good, because a lot of the same faces returned. More surprising was the considerable number of women who showed up, and of course, I had no problem with that. The arrangement was good, Lacey and I were able to spend more time together and make some money.

Everything was good for nine months, and then tragedy struck. One evening Lacey and I were returning from a two-day road trip at two am. I exited the interstate and was only two blocks from my apartment when the streets behind me lit up with blue lights. I was nervous, so I panicked. Without thinking, my foot pushed heavy on the gas pedal and the vehicle jumped forward. I was leading the cops on a high-speed chase out of fear. Fear of being arrested, and the fear of losing my girl.

I made a few clever turns, but I couldn't shake the police. I told her that there was no sense in the both of us going to jail, and that she should bail out. I slowed the car slightly and she acted reluctant. There was no time to discuss what had to be done, so I leaned across the passenger's seat, opened the door, and pushed her out into the street.

As I sped away, I watched in the rearview mirror as she landed awkwardly on the side of the curb. When I looked ahead, the road was blocked by police vehicles. A police helicopter hovered overhead with its searchlights enveloping the car. I slammed on the brakes and the car screeched to a stop. I put my hands in the air as they approached with their guns aimed steady and trigger fingers stiff. They pulled me from the car and slammed me on the ground before handcuffing me. I was thrown in the back of a police cruiser and they read me my rights.

While I watched the drama unfold from the back of the police cruiser, I hoped that Lacey had gotten away. That dream shattered when I saw her being escorted by one officer to another officer, who looked her over before putting her in his car. The arresting officer walked over to me, and with much excitement he explained to me how he had found my accomplice. He talked about how pretty she was and said that he understood how she would bring in the money that she did.

I stayed in the county jail for two weeks. While out on bond I avoided Lacey. I knew she was around, but I couldn't risk seeing her, for fear of falling in love again. I still loved her, but in light of everything, I thought it best to end our love affair. Evidently, she took offense to this, because during my trial she worked on the behalf of the prosecutor. I was sentenced to one year in jail.

In jail, she came to visit me a few times, and I told her there were no hard feelings. I also told her that even though I appreciated her visits at the moment, when I was released our relationship was over. She was indifferent regarding the situation and still visited a few times after that.

When I finished my sentence, I focused on living a life without my first love. After about three months' time, I began to feel confident that I could do it. From time to time she would show up at various places in the community. As before, she was always the life of any party she attended, and still as beautiful as ever. She kept a new love interest, and whoever she was with always seemed happy. I know that if I wanted her back in my life, she would be with me.

Last I heard, she is still a great dancer, and has danced under the stage names of Mary Jane, La-La, and other aliases. Her legacy is renowned, and her promiscuousness is alluring. If one should cross paths with her, I urge you to use caution. Marijuana, can't live with her, can't live without her.

FOCAL POINT

Jacob didn't know if he and his wife would make it to see their seventh year of marriage. For the last two years their lives had been filled with tribulation. Their days had been burdened with miscommunications and disagreements. They had a big blow out the night before. Neither one of them had made it to pick up their daughter from her violin classes. Each blamed the other, a shouting match ensued, and when it was all said and done, Jacob ended up sleeping on the couch. He had been sleeping on the couch so much over the last year that the cushions were permanently indented with his sleep print.

Jacob's alarm woke him up, he picked up his phone from off the coffee table and killed the alarm. He lay on the couch, listening, waiting to hear his wife get in the shower. When he heard the showers, he dashed into the bedroom and pulled his suit from the closet. He had been getting dressed for work in the living room and grooming in the guest bathroom as of late. They were trying to stay out each other's way as much as possible. He got dressed, and before he was set to leave, his wife came from the bedroom dressed in her robe. She walked to the kitchen and didn't bother to glance in his direction. Jacob threw on his knit top coat and scarf, he pulled his wool hat on his head haphazardly and left the house. On his way out, he slammed the door, just loud enough for her to hear.

It was cold outside, 22 degrees, the side walk was still icy from the previous week's snow. He buttoned his coat up tight to the last button, threw his scarf around his throat, pulled his cap tight, put his head down, and began the short trek to the bus stop. He couldn't believe how far apart he and his wife had grown. It had been a gradual process though, and no matter what he tried, he couldn't stop the downward spiral. He knew that he still loved her, but the fighting had become paralyzing. They were reaching the end of their 30s and he was beginning to feel the strain of the emotional distress, both physically and mentally. If he was drained, he knew she had to feel it too.

Up ahead of him, at the cross street about 40 yards away, he could see the back of a man in a tan trench coat waiting to board a bus at the bus stops. Coming up behind the man, Jacob could see something dangling from the man's coat pocket. At first, Jacob thought it was a pair of gloves, but then, after a third glance, it looked more like a wallet. Whatever it was, it was about to drop from the unsuspecting person's pocket. The closer he got, the surer he became that it was a wallet. Jacob had lost his wallet before. He knew the rest of the day was going to be miserable for the guy once he realized he had lost his wallet.

He heard the bus before he saw it. It was clear to Jacob that as soon as the guy took the first step on to the bus, the wallet would fall. Jacob wanted to help, he picked up his pace, but the bus was already pulling up to the stop. He quickened his pace but didn't want to move too fast and slip on a patch of black ice.

"Hey!" he called out, hoping to get the person's attention. That didn't work. The bus stopped and opened its doors. Jacob was still 30 feet away as the passengers began to get on. Jacob yelled out again, but the man continued to board. Just as his foot lifted onto the first step, Jacob watched as the wallet fell from his pocket, landing in a pile of black slush.

The bus sputtered off just as Jacob arrived. He quickly scooped up the wallet, which he immediately recognized wasn't a wallet at all, it was an eyeglasses case. He held the case high and waved it in the air, hoping that the bus driver would catch a glimpse of him and his flailing arms in the rear-view window. To no avail, the bus rolled on down the street, on schedule. Jacob looked down at the eyeglass case in his hands, he shook off the slush before putting the case in his pocket and darting to his bus stop just in time to catch his bus to work.

On the bus, his mind immediately resorted back to his family. He didn't want to leave his daughter—at 12 years old she was at her most crucial years for grooming. She didn't deserve to have to witness her parents quarrel like kids, on a daily basis. He popped his ear buds in his ears and listened to old school love songs the entire 20-minute long ride to the job, hoping to find answers to his problems in the lyrics.

At work, Jacob walked into his office and hung his coat on the back of his office door. He sat down at his desk and clasped his hands behind his head while he spent a few moments reflecting on his marriage. There was empty space on his office desk next to his office phone where he had taken down the picture of he and his wife. As it stood, he was done trying; it was time to move on. His first order of business was to find a place to live.

He started his computer to begin his apartment search on-line. Before his computer came on, he remembered the eye glasses case. He got up and went and got the case from his coat pocket. As he walked back to his desk, he examined the case in detail. The case was of premiere quality, made with rich black leather. It looked to be handmade and hand stitched. You could smell the robust leather throughout the small office. Jacob sat back down behind the desk and opened the case.

Resting on the cases red velvet lining were a pair of black, square framed glasses. The lenses were thick and lightly tinted black. His initial intention was to find a return label on the inside, but he was immediately drawn to the assembly of the glasses. He stared at the frames quizzically. He could tell by the quality of the case, and by the construction of the glasses themselves that this was an expensive pair of spectacles.

He found no return labeling on, or in the case. He officially had no way to return the glasses to their owner. He fiddled with the glasses a moment and his brain migrated back to the issues he was having with his wife. Money wasn't an issue, housing wasn't issue. It was communication that was an issue. It had been hard to come to an agreement on things. They couldn't even plan their family vacation for the coming summer because they couldn't agree on where to go. Their daughter had recently began playing the violin, like her mother suggested. He thought she should be playing the clarinet. His wife was always right, though. At least she thought she was. When the computer finally loaded, Jacob put the glasses back into their case and began his work day.

Jacob zoned out in his work. Developing housing blue prints had always been therapeutic for him. Once he started building, his mind was free of all worries. At lunchtime, Jacob reached for his cell phone. He looked to see if his wife had text him to say something, anything. He thought that maybe he should text her something, something nice, maybe even send chocolate strawberries to her job. It was hard to be nice to someone who wasn't nice to you, though. There was nothing on his phone from her. He pushed away from the desk, and out of his peripheral view he spotted the eyeglasses case. He grabbed it and put it in his coat pocket before leaving his office for lunch.

He didn't really have an appetite, so he decided to take a walk in the city park across from where his office building was. He followed the paved path through the park. He did this when he wanted to clear his mind; he had been essentially taking this walk every day for the past year. That's how rocky a relationship he and his wife was having.

He came to a small, rickety bridge and took a moment to stop and stare over the side off into the distance, his eyes following the creek's trail as far he could see. Instinctively, he thought about the glasses he had in his pocket. He wondered just how far down the creeks trail he could see if he put the glasses on. He pulled the case from his pocket and eyed the frames skeptically. He didn't want to damage his vision by wearing a stranger's glasses, but he didn't plan on wearing them long. They were so upscale, he assumed that they could even be fashion glasses. He stared into the front of the lenses for a moment before turning the glasses around and placing them on his face.

Then he began to see.

He was standing behind the guy who had lost his glasses while getting on the bus. Jacob knew it was him because of his coat. He was just getting home to his quaint townhome. Inside he made his way to the kitchen, and found his wife sitting at the dining room table with a glass of wine. Her eyes lit up when she seen him. He kissed her and slid into the chair across from her and held both her hands in his own. They bowed their heads and prayed. They had a conversation after that. They laughed, and in that same moment the wife cried. He got up and pulled her into his chest, and she rested her head there for a while. Then, hand in hand, they headed up the stairs. At the top of the stairs, they stood at the threshold of the first door on the right. They stared into the room, like when you watch your child sleep. Then, bravely, they stepped inside.

Inside the room their daughter was there sleeping. Her room was decorated in pink. Pink curtains, pink bed spreads and rugs. Their daughter looked to be about 12 years old. She was resting peacefully on her back with her eyes closed; her braids splayed out on the pink pillow casing. Light perspiration dotted her forehead and her cinnamon shaded complexion was chalky. Her hands were down by her sides, and an IV ran up her left hand, along her arm, along the mattress, before coiling at the end of the IV bag.

They walked up to the bedside and they took turns kissing her cheek. There were two chairs arranged at the side of the bed and they took their seats. They talked to each other and to the daughter. She couldn't respond, but they talked to her as if she could. After a while, the mother began to read from a book she picked up from off the night stand. The father found a space on the floor and listened to his wife read with his head propped up on a pillow. Awhile later, his wife joined him on the floor and they played card games. All the while, they engaged their daughter, although she didn't respond, they still communicated with her as if she could.

Then night fell. The husband and wife stood up. They took turns saying good night to their daughter before holding hands and leaving for their bedroom.

Jeff snatched the glasses off and gave them an aporetic stare. He put them back on and couldn't see a thing, the medicine in the lenses was blinding. He snatched them off and then looked around the park as if he was being spied on. He pulled his phone from his pocket and looked at the time, only six minutes had passed. He looked at the glasses again. Fear made him want to toss them in the creek below.

It was times like this when he longed for his wife's companionship. This was something he wanted to share, but who would believe him. Not even his wife would believe him, but at least she would take him seriously. He needed to get back to the office, he was dizzy and needed to sit down.

As soon as he took his first step, he missed his footing and stumbled violently to the right, his momentum made him crash into the bridges railing. His full body weight smashing into the rail, caused it to splinter violently. The railing could not support his weight, it gave way and he fell the few feet into the small creek below, landing hard on the rocks and stream of water.

He hopped up quickly, the frigid temperatures from the creek water had snatched his breath away. His feet and entire right side was soaked. He frantically stumbled out of the creek and up the slight embankment towards the path, embarrassed and confused. When he got back on the path, he took a moment to regain his composure. The shock of the fall and the freezing temperatures had jolted him back to reality. He found his footing, then he swiftly headed back to the office.

His mind was whirling with thoughts as he walked. He kept looking over his shoulder like he was being followed. He didn't think he was crazy, but he had just encountered the most mysterious event he had ever confronted. He had vividly seen into another man's life as if he had been watching a movie. He walked back to his office in a blur, he was still trying to conceptualize what he had just seen through the glasses. He didn't know what was more appalling, having the vision, or what he saw in the vision.

He was so entangled in his thoughts that when he came to the cross street across from his office building, he didn't even stop, he walked directly out into the passing traffic. A black SUV came to a screeching halt only inches away from him.

The driver of the SUV lay into his horn and yelled obscenities as Jacob hustled on across the street to the embarrassing blare of the car horns. Jacob could only imagine how he had looked. A bewildered man soaked in freezing creek water, wandering out into traffic.

He burst through the revolving doors of his office building and bolted to the closest stairway. He took the eight flights of stairs swiftly, and when he made it to the eighth floor he hurried down the hall before disappearing into his office unseen.

Inside the office he closed and locked the door before pulling the blinds tight. He quickly pulled off his coat and hung the damp garment on the back of the door. He pulled off his wet pants and shoes and placed them near the radiator. In his boxer shorts, he hurried into his bathroom and stared at himself in the mirror. His dress shirt was wet and stained and he had small traces of moss in his low Caesar haircut. He fanned at the moss irritated. He was beginning to warm up a bit. He thought about his wife and daughter. He thought about the family he had seen in the vision.

Then he remembered that he hadn't checked for his phone since he had fallen. He burst back into his office and picked up his pants from off the floor near the radiator. He checked the pockets. He didn't feel his phone. He rushed over to the door where his coat hung. In the first pocket that he checked, he felt his phone. There were no messages from his wife and no phone calls. He pulled up her name and began to text. He could see her last text to him had been from nine days earlier, and it simply read, "whatever."

"I really need to talk to you," he texted.

He stared at the phone for a few seconds, then he sat down in his office chair and lay the phone down on the desk. He put his head back on the leather and closed his eyes. He could hear his heart beating in his head. The last 20 minutes of his life had been rousing to say the least. As his heart begin to slow he began to understand.

Suddenly, he opened his eyes and sat up. Where were the glasses? He got up fast and raced to his coat. He checked the front pockets of the jacket, and then the interior ones. No glasses. He checked his pants pockets again. No glasses. He went into the bathroom. Still, no glasses. He thought back to when he had last seen them. It had been right before he fell into the creek. He walked over to the office window and looked down into the street below. He was almost certain that he had dropped them somewhere between the fall and the walk to the office.

He fell back into his office chair after a moment and reached for his phone. His wife had text back. "We can talk," she had replied.

Jeff smiled at the response. He hadn't really expected a response, but he had gotten one. He couldn't wait to talk to his wife, it had been a long time since they had a conversation. He had a lot to talk about. He reached in his bottom desk drawer and pulled out the framed photo of he and her. He positioned it back on the desk, where it had been for the last seven years.

WORK

I hit the free world bricks with high expectations. I had a plan that had been thoroughly masterminded for an entire year of having nothing else to do, but plan. The bus ride home was the grandest journey I had ever taken. Shackle free, handcuff free. I even looked at my wrist just to make sure I wasn't dreaming. The sun was shining this fall morning, but you could still smell the remnants of summer. The bus ride was quiet, maybe because it was early and most everyone was sleep. Not me though, I was up like a ceiling fan.

I watched the scenery pass as the bus sped down the interstate headed for the inner city. The bus ride previous to this one had been on a prison bus. On that bus you can only view the scenery through wire mesh. You have to squint very hard to see through those windows. Still, I had seen bloody battles about a window seat. Prison was real like that.

I had distinct plans about my future. I pulled my release check from my pocket and read it again as if for the first time. It was worth 150 dollars. Not a lot to give a man just released from the can. One hundred and twenty-five of those dollars was what I managed to save over the years. As soon as the bus dropped me off downtown, I cashed my check at the first liquor store I saw. I bought a beer and a pack of cigarettes.

I left the store and walked a few blocks. I found a dumpster in an alley, hid behind it, and downed the beer in about seven gulps. I spent my buzz walking around the city. Things had changed. There were new buildings, new faces, but a lot of the same faces. People looked at me like they recognized me, and they did. They recognized me by the brown paper bag I carried balled up under my arm, and by my attire. My khakis were stiff, and my white dress shirt was heavy on the polyester, but the Chuck Taylor's sneakers were official. My clothes screamed prison release. I stopped at a bodega two blocks away from my old neighborhood. I sat my bag down and fired up a cigarette.

I was two pulls in when two of the older dudes from my neighborhood came to the store, Sammy and Jesse. They were both about 45 years old, and I don't think they had ever been outside the city limits. The next city over was only about 20 minutes away, but these two couldn't tell you anything about it. Jessie stayed with his mother. Sammy stayed with one of his baby mommas. Sammy is Puerto Rican and had a way with the ladies; he had four kids and two baby mommas. Jesse was the best fighter on the block, had been for years. He drank too much, but it didn't affect his boxing skills. The both of them found solace in the neighborhood and all its ghetto antics. These two were permanent fixtures in the neighborhood, as permanent as pawnshops and beat cops.

As soon as they recognized me they grew excited, someone being released from prison was just as grand an event as high school graduation. Jesse was the first to recognize me; he smiled a jagged tooth smile and said, "Malachi, when you got out lil homey?"

I found it hard not to look at his teeth. He had either aged or finally lost a fight, maybe two. "Today," I said.

"Damn, I see you was doing pushups in that camp," Sammy said. "You think you can whoop Jesse's ass now?"

Sammy was forever the instigator. Whereas Jesse was undefeated, Sammy had never won a fight.

"Oh, you think you got skills Malachi?" Jesse said, already throwing up his boxing set.

I shook my head and flicked the cigarette to the curb. "I don't want any problems, Jesse. I know you the champ."

"And don't forget it either," Jesse shot back. He and Sammy ventured into the store, laughing, amused that even before they had their breakfast beer, something exciting had occurred in the neighborhood.

I knew I didn't want to be like them when I was 30, let alone 45 years old. At 24 I had already resolved that by the time I was 30, I would be successful in my own rite. Beamer, Benz, or Bentley.

While I walked the final blocks to my mother's home, I noticed that while a lot had changed, a lot of things hadn't. My neighborhood was made up of decrepit buildings of clay-stained brick where suspicious characters loomed on the street corners. I entered my building and took the stairs two at a time up to my mother's apartment. She answered the door after the first knock, like she had been standing at the door with her hand on the knob. "Malachi!" she exclaimed. She grabbed me and embraced me. She was crying and genuinely excited to have me home.

It took a good 20 minutes for her to finally accept that I was free. She was amused by the fact that we could finally talk for as long as we liked without being supervised by uniformed guards, and at the end of the conversation, I would still be around.

We sat at the kitchen table where she had prepared lunch. She couldn't stop smiling at me from across the table. For the next two hours, we talked about what was going on in the city, those who passed, and those who went to prison. We talked about who was off drugs and who had started using again. Then she finally asked the question that I knew she would ask.

"Now that you're out, what are your plans?"

I was scared to open my eyes when I awoke the next day. I didn't want to open my eyes and still be in prison. The twin size mattress that I slept on, although small, was a million times more comfortable than a prison mat. In the bathroom I took off my wave cap and brushed the thick layer of well-groomed waves I had trained over the last three years. I closed my eyes and splashed my face with warm water. While my eyes were closed, I remembered the previous evening's conversation with my mother. I had spent a good portion of that evening telling her all the things she wanted to hear; you know, the spill about jobs and responsibilities.

Getting out of prison means starting over. Before I went in I owned a car and had my own place. Now, I only had 150 dollars to my name. It was imperative that I get my plans underway. I dressed in the same get up as the day before and left the house.

I headed two blocks east to see an old friend. When I arrived, I noticed Steady's silver Mercedes E-class parked out front of his apartment building. It wasn't the same Mercedes he owned before I went in, but a newer model. I knew it belonged to him because of the car's tag. It read, "ST-MONEY". That stood for steady money. Steady stayed on the first floor, first door on the right, the same residence for as long as I had known him.

I knocked on the door seven times before he finally answered. He opened the door, looked me up and down, and then grinned before saying, "Malachi! When you get out!?" He clutched the heavy gold chain that hung from his neck out of habit. We slapped hands.

"What up, Steady? I got out yesterday, had to spend the first day with mom, feel me?"

"I feel you." He looked me up and down again, and I could tell that he was happy I was home. "Well, come on in and have a sit down. I was just about to pour up some Hennessey. You being home is a definite reason to take a shot."

The two-bedroom apartment was in a low-income area, but the inside was furnished as exquisitely as any penthouse suite on the North Side. The pad was busy with the latest in flat screens and gaming systems. Leather couches and barstools calmed things down a taste. The place was comfortably arranged. Too well put together for any man to coordinate by himself. Sitting at the barstool, I anticipated that he had a girlfriend. He poured us up two shots on the counter. He grabbed his chain and raised his shot glass to the roof. "Here's to being back on them streets," he said before tossing back the liquid.

I threw mine back and we did it again, because getting out of prison is celebrated in my neighborhood. Like when soldiers return from war.

Moments after the second shot was when I noticed the most prized of Steady's possessions. Samantha. She was wearing Yoga pants and a tight T-shirt. She was curvy, voluptuous, and had the face of a model. High cheek bones, radiant cocoa complexioned skin, and a stylishly short haircut. I hadn't been around women for years, only seeing Samantha made me realize how long it had been.

"I want a shot," she said playfully giddy while dancing around the bar top.

"You got it baby," Steady said, kissing her on the cheek.

When she looked at me, I realized that I had been staring at her the entire time.

"What's your name?" she asked.

"Malachi," I replied.

"Malachi just got out," Steady began. "He did five years, that's why we taking shots." He filled up a shot glass and slid it to her.

She looked at me and said, "Here's to you." She tossed back the shot, but her eyes never left mine. When she was done, she winked and smiled before waltzing back to the bedroom.

"So did you come over here looking for a job lead? Or did you come to get some work?" He asked when she was gone.

"I came to get some work," I said flatly.

"Well then, you came to the right place," he said while heading over to the ceramic canisters arranged on the counter top. He removed the lid to the one labeled 'flour'. He reached into the jar and removed a bag. "I got a little welcome home present for you." He reached in and pulled out a sandwich bag one fourth of the way filled with cocaine. "You still remember how to whip?"

"That's like riding a bike, big homey," I said, reaching into my pockets for the money to pay him. "I only got like one fifty."

He shook his head. "Malachi, why would you insult me like that? You just got back. This is on the house baby."

Already things were looking up. I had a hustle, and a little pocket change. I spent the remainder of the afternoon in the mall. Prices had risen since I left, only inspiring me to get back on my feet as soon as possible. I left the mall with a new fit and zero dollars in my pocket. I made it home by three pm, and my mom wasn't expected home from her job until six o clock. I opened a couple windows, then rushed into the kitchen and pulled out the largest pot from underneath the kitchen sink. I hated to resort to cooking up dope in my mom's kitchen, but this was the only time, I swore on that.

I spent the better half of 30 minutes boiling and mixing. I used a razor blade to cut up the finished product into small unique squares to be sold at 10 dollars a bit. Before my arrest, I would only sell ounces. It was easy for me to want to get back in the drug trade, it had never let me down.

When I was done cooking, I had 500 hundred dollars' worth of sales to make. I stashed half of the dope in the toe of my old prison sneaker, changed my clothes, and left the apartment.

I bought a newspaper from the corner store and sat on one of the benches out front. It was a nice day, sunny, and the temperature was perfect with a complimentary breeze every so often. In the early afternoon things were slow, a few of the high school kids stopped in the store to buy cigars to roll up their marijuana.

Others spent a moment on the bench to hold their cell phone conversations. I read a little, I even breezed through the job section. I didn't see much there. I smoked a cigarette. I went into the store and bought a soda.

Then, finally, something of interest occurred. A guy walked up and I overheard his cell phone conversation. Whereas a lot of things had changed, the slang was still the same. I heard him say, "You know I stay with it."

A time was set, and a meeting place arranged. He and the caller had agreed to meet on the corner of Fourteenth and K Street. I knew exactly where that was, while he was still on the phone I headed in that direction.

On K Street the foot traffic was heavy; I could sense that this was an area high in drug interchange. I spent the next several hours being observant, and even witnessed some discreet exchanges that would be invisible to the naked eye, but I knew what to look for. It was the covert glances up and down the streets. The conversations in which neither party looked at the other for fear of taking their eyes from their block surveillance. Drug task force agents like to appear as if from the skies, as quickly and unannounced as summer showers.

Users and sellers don't look alike, in any transaction you can tell who's using and who's selling. Sellers are the more cautious individuals. Users are more hurried with their actions. They pace, they looked concerned, they look desperate in most cases. When I spotted one lone gentleman pacing with other identifiable user qualities, I asked what he was looking for, to which he replied, "Are you working?"

Word traveled fast, and by the end of the day I had made eight sales. I was generous with my supply, and the users appreciated this. An old school player in the Penn told me that it's not how much you make off one sell, it's how fast you sell that turns the profit. Within the next two days, sales doubled. A week from then I was feeling like my old drug dealing self again. I felt sharper out there in the streets, I guess because during my three-year sentence I had revised how I would approach the dope game this time around.

After being out of prison for only three weeks, I was

fast in route to reestablishing myself in the neighborhood. I was pulling in close to 1500 dollars a week. One morning my mom woke me up and called me to the kitchen for breakfast. She was in her work uniform. A green maid's uniform complete with apron. I sat down at the table and she slid eggs straight from the skillet onto my plate.

"So tell me about this job again?" she said.

I lifted a fork full of eggs to my mouth and began to chew. I hated to lie to my mother but… "I found a job at little clothing store in the mall. I've been training about a week. I think I'm about to be hired permanently," I lied expertly.

She dropped the pan into the sink and turned to me with her eyes beaming her pride. "I'm so happy you're sticking to your plans, Malachi, because if you stick to your plans you will succeed."

It was time to replenish my supply. I was doing this on a weekly basis now, sometimes twice a week. I stopped by Steady's house late in the afternoon. Samantha opened the door with the chain attachment still engaged. She spoke through a minor crack in the doors opening. "What's up?" she asked groggily, like she had just woken up.

"Steady home?"

"No, why, you need something?"

"Yeah, its re-up time."

"Ok, hold on for a second," she replied before closing the door and unlocking the chain. She opened the door, and the sunlight from the hallway cast a glow on her silhouette as she stood in the dim lit apartment. She was wearing only lingerie, lacey, explicit in its cut, and provocative in design. "You just going to stand there and stare or are you going to come in?"

I stood there in silence caught up in a lustful stupor. It took her almost closing the door in my face for me to respond.

"No, I'm sorry. I'm coming in," I replied, entering and finding a place to sit on the sofa. I began to wonder if she was trying to seduce me. I quickly resolved that I was overreacting, possibly in her hurry to answer the door she hadn't a chance to put on at least a robe. She reappeared shortly afterwards, and she hadn't added any article of clothing, destroying my only hypothesis as to why she was dressed in only lingerie.

She dropped a neatly folded and tapped brown paper bag on the glass coffee table in front of me. "Is that all?" she said with her hands planted on her well-proportioned hips.

I swallowed hard and replied, "I think so."

She licked her lips seductively and smiled. She was amused by my discomfort. Her lips were glossy, I was almost sure they weren't that shiny when she first answered the door. I grabbed the work off the table and headed for the door. I grabbed the door handle and she said, "How does it feel to go all that time without having sex?"

Without out looking back I replied, "It's the hardest thing in the world." Outside, I inhaled deeply; it was like I had been holding my breath the entire time I was inside.

One month later, things were working in my favor. I had saved up some money. I bought an Acura and threw some rims and tint on it. My wardrobe was nothing but the exclusive in design. Gucci sneakers, Louie Vuitton belts. My pockets stayed bulging with a hustler's bankroll. Most important of all, I hadn't made any enemies yet; you know how feisty the haters can get.

I kept most of my material possessions in the trunk of my car so that I wouldn't have to explain my elaborate purchases to my mother. I still played the role of being employed. I woke up at eight o clock on most mornings and left as if I had a real job.

I was growing tired of this routine, so I knew that my next venture would involve getting my own place. Now more than ever, I had developed a desire for female companionship. Having my own apartment, I knew would make that task less daunting. Samantha didn't help the situation. Several times since her first advances she had either acted or said inappropriate things. It even seemed as if she knew or anticipated when it was time for me to re-up, because every time that I did, Steady was nowhere to be found. I told myself that it was wrong for me to dwell on the explicit thoughts that coursed my mind, like sucking on her bottom lip, or grasping a handful of her pillow soft ass. I warned myself that if I ever gave in to her advances, that would be a direct deviation from all that I had planned, and I didn't need those problems.

It was re-up time again. I knocked on Steady's door and crossed my fingers, hoping that he would be home, even though I didn't notice his car parked anywhere out front. I hoped Samantha had borrowed the car and was gone. The idea was farfetched, but I needed to re-up, there was money to make. To my dismay, it wasn't the baldheaded, dark skinned Steady who answered the door. It was his extremely better half, Samantha. She was wearing a long, curve hugging black dress complete with splits on either side that ran up her legs. Every time that she moved, the splits would offer a glimmer of her chocolate thighs. There was soft music playing lowly throughout, scented candles created a sensually aromatic atmosphere. She held a glass of champagne in her hand. "Hey Malachi, come on in," she said leaving the door open and heading for the kitchen.

"Where's Steady?" I called, closing the door before taking a seat on the couch.

"He had to drive to Florida, but he should be back tomorrow," she said. I could hear the chime of glasses as she prepared something. Seconds later, she appeared with an extra champagne glass filled to the brim. "Ace of Spades," she said, handing me the glass of bubbly.

I accepted the drink. She sat down right next to me and crossed her legs; her naked thighs creamy and athletic. "I'm going to need the usual," I said, fighting the urge to touch her legs, to kiss her. She wanted me to, I could tell.

"That's cool," she replied. "It's going to cost you a little extra this time though."

"Why, there's a drought or something?"

"No, no drought."

"Why the extra?" I asked. Then, without warning, she grabbed my crotch and began to massage my erection. "Hold on Samantha," I said, removing her hand. I took my champagne and downed the entire glass in one smooth gulp. I grimaced from the effort, put down my glass, and without another second to pass I kissed her aggressively.

She was a little shocked, but responded with the same fervor as I. Our tongues danced and twirled in and out of each other's mouths. She stood up and removed the straps of her dress and let it drop to the floor. I sat on the couch, looking up at her hour glass figure. She grabbed my hand and led me to the bedroom, my eyes following the cadent sway of her buttocks.

Twenty minutes later, I sat on the edge of the bed and fixed my clothing while Samantha lay there caught up in her own thoughts. I felt bad that I had slept with Steady's girl, but how much could a man take? I looked over at her and she was almost sleeping. I stood up and buckled my belt. "So, what's supposed to happen now?" I asked.

She sat up and pulled the covers to her chin before, shrugging her shoulders. "I'll be around," she said. She nodded towards the dresser. "Your work is over there."

I walked over to the dresser, picked up the folded brown paper bag, dropped a role of money in its place. "I guess I'll see you around," I said.

"Maybe," she replied, laying back into her pillows.

I stared at her expecting more, but that was all. I pulled on my jacket and put the work in an inner pocket before closing the bedroom door on my way out. I left the apartment, and no sooner had I stepped outside than my heart shifted upwards in my chest. Steady's car was parked right out front, and then out of nowhere Steady was standing directly in front of me. The suddenness of his appearance was so unexpected that I jumped at the sight of him. "Steady. What you doing here?" I asked, the words tumbling from my mouth against my will.

"I live here Malachi, you high or something?"

"I'm cool. Samantha just told me you were out of town and I didn't expect to see you."

"Did she take care of you?"

"Yeah," I said, patting my jacket pocket where I had stashed the work.

He placed a hand on my shoulder and said, "Let's ride up to the sports bar and have a drink. Talk about how you coming along in the game. You have been out what, three months now?"

"Yeah about that," I said while mentally reliving the sexual romp with Samantha only a few short minutes before. I figured that by agreeing to drinks, it would at least buy her some time. "Drinks sound cool."

Inside the car I relaxed in the leather interiors of Steady's Benz. We rode without conversation for a few minutes; to say that I felt weird would be an understatement. It was just a little bit too close for comfort that Steady had appeared when he had. I knew that he could detect that I was nervous when he spoke to me. Sometimes you can just smell when confrontation is brewing. Prison familiarizes you with this distinct stench. It reeked now.

We were traveling down a four-lane highway; we passed eateries and shopping centers along either side of us. Traffic was light this afternoon. Steady reached across me and unlatched the glove compartments. He pulled out a bulky black nine-millimeter. I watched him with lurid anticipation of what was next, I had just slept with his girlfriend.

He stared at the traffic ahead of us with the gun gripped in his right hand then said, "Malachi, I knew Samantha was sleeping with somebody, but I never thought…" he stopped talking and shook his head in despondence. "Not you Malachi, not you." He finished. "That's why this is going to hurt me even more. I'm losing my girl and a friend," he said, stopping at a red light.

I couldn't believe what I was hearing. I looked at Steady to try and gauge how serious he was. His eyes were watering. He pulled the slide of the gun, and I took that as my cue. I opened the car door and darted in the opposite direction.

I started off in a slight jog, not really expecting for him to get out of the vehicle and chase me, but he did. He chased me down the highway with his gun openly exposed. He had lost all sanity. I broke out into an all-out run motivated by fear. He fired off a shot, and everything I had done since being released coursed my mind.

I dodged moving cars and side stepped parked ones. I cut left for the sidewalk, and he was right behind me. I could see the astonished faces of some drivers as I ran in search of a safe haven. What I didn't know was that one of the on lookers was an unmarked police car. I ran to a gas station and tried to go in. The teller had been watching the chase and had already locked the doors. The brief stop took precious seconds off my lead, and the next thing I knew Steady had grabbed me by the lapel of my jacket. I came out of the jacket swiftly and was headed back for the highway when a police cruiser pulled directly in front of me. I ran straight up onto the hood of the car, lost my footing, and fell onto the concrete.

The officer hopped out with his gun drawn and screamed, "Don't move!" His gun barrel was only inches from my nose. Another police car pulled up, and while I was told to lie on my stomach and put my hands behind my head, I saw my leather jacket lying on the ground next to the store's door, but no Steady. While the familiar feel of handcuffs gripped my wrist, I watched as another officer walked over and picked up the jacket. He held it up so that the store attendant could see it, the clerk pointed at me. The officer searched the jacket right there on the spot. I closed my eyes because I didn't want to witness him make the discovery.

"Is this your jacket?" a voice asked. I refused to answer. I knew my rights at least, anything they needed to know they could find out on their own. I chuckled on the inside; I thought I had covered everything while planning in prison, but this was something I couldn't prepare for.

It was the hardest thing in the world to pick up the phone and call my mother from the county jail and attempt to explain. She cried the entire call, and for the first time I realized that when planning you have to consider everyone involved. I hadn't planned on hurting my mother's feelings the way that I had. Still, she was present at all my court hearings. Seeing her disappointment was more depressing than the four-year sentence I received for cocaine possession.

Steady was never arrested. No charges, no evidence that he was even a part of the incident. I lay on the top bunk of my cell and reminisced about the small twin size bed at my mother's home. I missed my freedom. I had four years to devise a new plan, and I vowed to plan differently. Drug dealing wasn't for me.

Three months after my conviction, I was on a prison bus on my way back to prison. My wrists were cuffed and my ankles were shackled. It was hard to see the passing scenery due to the wire mesh that covered the window.

Please leave a review @amazon.com
Thank you.
Yourstoryhere.biz

Shawn Powell